A CORNISH REVENGE

A bleak Cornish clifftop strewn with the derelict remains of old tin mines seems to magazine editor Loveday Ross an odd place for an art class; her artist friend Lawrence Kemp has been acting strangely recently. As Loveday takes the pictures she needs for an article, a grim sight emerges as the tide recedes below. It's the body of a man who, Loveday realises with horror, was deliberately left to drown. But why has the discovery, awful though it is, affected Lawrence and his students so deeply?

RENA GEORGE

♦

A CORNISH REVENGE

Complete and Unabridged

LINFORD
Leicester

First published in Great Britain

First Linford Edition
published 2014

A catalogue record for this book is available
from the British Library.

ISBN 978–1–4448–2086–7

Published by
F. A. Thorpe (Publishing)
Anstey, Leicestershire

Prologue

He stood between the fluted pillars of the big granite villa; a small, dapper man in a dark silk shirt and matching needle cord trousers. His grey eyes narrowed as he watched his wife's red MG disappear down the drive. Magdalene was off to meet her lover! She thought he didn't know. How stupid was that? Paul Bentine knew *everything* about the people in his life. That was where his power lay.

He grimaced after the retreating car, listening until the purr of its engine faded before turning back to his study. He pulled the crumpled paper from his pocket and smoothed it out on his desk. The letters had been clipped from a newspaper. It was a tabloid. He flicked the grubby sheet across the desk and narrowed his eyes. It was shoddy, incompetent, amateurish rubbish — and bloody insulting if anybody actually believed he could be intimidated by it.

Reaching for his brandy glass he swirled the amber liquid before raising it to his lips. '*Your Time Has Come!*' the note had said. He threw back the contents of the glass in one gulp and smirked. It was some pathetic attempt to rattle him, but it wasn't working. Lawyers got threatened all the time, it was the nature of the job . . . and with his little sideline . . .

But this was the third note. The first had arrived in the mail eight days earlier. '*I Know What You've Been Doing!*' It was followed four days later by the second stark message. '*I'm Watching You!*'

Taking them to the police was not an option. He didn't want any flat-footed coppers ferreting about in his business, but he hadn't destroyed them either. The vile thing on his desk now would join the others, locked away in his safe box on the boat. He'd pondered the sense of keeping them at first, but his legal mind had persuaded him not to destroy potentially valuable evidence. Besides . . . they might even come in useful, once he had discovered who sent them — and he would.

Discovering things about people — things he could use to his advantage — was what Paul Bentine did best.

Did his beautiful, rich wife really believe he would not find out about her little liaisons with the amorous vicar? They were the mice and he was the cat . . . and what fun he would have with them. The thought made him smile. How righteous would the Rev Martin Foley seem in the eyes of his flock then? Bentine poured himself another brandy and savoured the thought of how much he would enjoy tormenting them, teasing out their misery, until it suited him to end their affair.

He went to the wall safe, took out the small black laptop and booted it up. They were all here, all the supreme mugs, the ones who had it all — until he made it his business to discover their seedy little secrets. He scrolled down the list. The names were impressive — a banker, the principal of a well known public school, a barrister, an artist, and two prominent company directors . . . all of them with something to hide.

The brandy bottle was empty now and he went in search of another. The computer was still open on his desk when he returned. He didn't hear the catch slide on the French windows behind him, or notice the soft footfall on the thick green carpet.

. . . But he felt the sharp pain as his arms were grabbed from behind, his wrists trussed together with a coarse twine, and a chloroform-soaked rag forced over his nose.

When he came round he was in total darkness, and for a moment he wondered if he was dead . . . But there was a noise . . . something familiar . . . he concentrated on it. It was the roar of car tyres on a tarmac road. He was moving. He was in a car . . . in the boot of a car. Suddenly, he couldn't breathe. He felt the panic rising. When he moved, there was a stab of pain across his shoulders and he realised that his hands were still tied behind him. His head throbbed. Pain was good. He could focus on pain.

The car stopped. There were muffled voices, then feet crunching gravel. What the hell was happening to him? The boot opened, but no light came in, only a rush of cold, damp air. Paul filled his lungs. He had no idea what time it was, not that it mattered, not if they were going to release him. He wondered if he was still in Cornwall. How easy would it be to find his way home?

Somewhere in the distance he could hear the sea . . . waves pounding rocks . . . he could taste the salt. A torch beam shone in his face.

'So, you're back with us?'

He'd heard the voice before . . . but when . . . where? He tried to think, to clear his mind, but everything was muddled. How did he know that voice?

'We're going for a little boat trip,' it said.

Rough hands grabbed him and yanked his body to a standing position. He swayed and the torch beam swung round — and Paul Bentine was looking into the eyes of his abductor.

'You! It's bloody you, isn't it?' he stared at the face he recognised. 'Why are you doing this? No, don't tell me.' Now that he knew the identity of his abductor it gave him power. 'OK, so you've got your own back. But your little joke has gone far enough. Now untie me!'

His gag was removed and the rope lashing his arms was sliced through. His hands were suddenly free. His wrists felt raw and he knew they were bleeding. He looked around and saw only blackness. 'You're not going to leave me out here in the middle of nowhere?' He tried to sound threatening, but the relief that filled his veins when he assumed he was being set free turned to chill when he saw the barrel of the gun.

'No Paul.' The voice was cold. 'You haven't yet served your purpose.'

He felt hands on his back and staggered as he was propelled along the sand. Was there more than one of them? He wasn't sure.

They stopped. And in the watery light of a half moon he made out the shape of a dinghy.

'Push the boat.' The order came with a sharp jab in the kidneys from the gun.

'Have you lost your mind?'

'I told you . . . we are going for a little trip, now do as you're told.'

Another jab.

Paul was long past arguing. He pushed, and felt the icy water flow around his ankles.

'Now get in and start the engine.'

He hated water . . . had an uncontrollable fear of it. He did, sometimes, secretly board Magdalene's boat in Falmouth marina, but even she knew better than to suggest that he should go sailing in it.

He was betting his captors knew that. Was this to be his punishment?

He stumbled on board, aware of the dark sea all around. Waves of nausea swept over him and he swiped at the beads of sweat on his forehead with a shaky hand. He was pushed into a corner and the engine sparked into life as they chugged away from shore into the blackness of the sea. He could see pinpoints of lights along the coast but they were too far out now to hope for help from that direction. He toyed with the idea of making a grab for the gun, but it might go off in his face. He wasn't that brave. Paul had no idea how far they had travelled before the order came to turn in to land. He got the impression of cliffs, then a patch of beach. The torch beam flashed again.

'Over there,' the voice commanded. 'Make for over there.'

It was a shingle cove, protected all around by the sheer black face of the cliffs. They beached the boat and climbed out. Then the order came.

'Strip off!'

'Are you mad? It's freezing. I've had enough of — '

But the moon slid from behind a cloud, and its silvery light picked out the glint of the gun barrel. It was pointing at him.

'Clothes off!' His kidnapper was getting agitated now.

Paul undressed, shivering, to his boxer shorts.

'Now down on your back'

Paul's eyes were wide with terror. He made one last desperate bid for mercy. 'If you want me to beg, then I'll beg. I'm sorry. Is that what you want to hear?' He was trembling. 'Look ... I made a mistake. I've admitted it ... And I'll keep my mouth shut about what's happened here tonight. I know you're only trying to frighten me — and I deserve it.' He waited for a response, but none came. '*Please*,' he pleaded into the darkness. 'Please let me go.'

He felt the cold steel of a gun barrel against his temple.

'Do as I say or it's a bullet in the head ... and at this range, I won't miss.'

He dropped to his knees and winced in pain as a push sent him splaying across the sharp shingle. His body tensed as a rope went round his wrist and was pegged into the grit. He screamed and tried to break free, then heard the cocking mechanism of the gun.

'OK. I'll do whatever you want ... just don't shoot me.'

He allowed his tormentor to peg down his other wrist and do the same with his ankles. He was now spread-eagled in this sinister cove. He could see the stars ... a whole heaven of stars so close above him. There was a crunch of feet on the shingle

. . . then the sound of an outboard springing to life. The dinghy was pulling away, chugging into the night.

At any moment he would see the flash of a camera . . . the giggle of those hiding amongst the rocks. Humiliation . . . that's what this was all about. He waited, but no sound came save for the noise of the waves. He could hear them lapping close now, feel the first sting of the icy sea as it reached the soles of his feet.

No one heard his screams. The water crept higher, moving up his legs . . . his torso . . . covering his chest. His eyes were wide with terror when it reached his neck. He fought frantically to free himself, but the pegs that held him down had been forced deep. He opened his mouth to scream again, but no sound came.

A tight pain flashed across Paul Bentine's chest before the darkness came down. The stars had gone!

1

Loveday Ross frowned at the glistening ribbon of wet road twisting ahead and tried to work out what was wrong with Lawrence.

The previous evening's exhibition in St Ives had been a triumph. At least five of his paintings had sold, which was wonderful because he'd made a point of inviting the county's most knowledgeable and discerning art critics and buyers. So why had he seemed so distracted?

She sighed, forcing her concentration back to the morning's picture shoot. Loveday was on her way to the old tin mine workings at Borlase, near Land's End. It was a bizarre place to hold an art class, particularly on a damp, grey Saturday in September. Images of pretty coves and villages, old harbours and standing stones, flitted through her mind. Any of these would have made a better picture spread for the magazine than the bleak landscape of brick chimney stacks and mine relics, but she trusted Lawrence. He knew what he was doing.

As she turned into the parking area, she glanced down at her green canvas satchel and went through a mental checklist — notebook, pens, digital recorder, camera. Her mobile phone was in her pocket. She got out, striding across the rough terrain, forcing the worry about her friend temporarily from her thoughts as she raised her camera and zoomed in on the old engine houses that clung precariously to the cliff-edge. They were an iconic Cornish image and she would be remiss not to include them in the article.

It had stopped raining, but the sea still looked hostile under the iron-grey sky. In spring and early summer these cliffs would be alive with nesting seabirds, and Loveday had been told that the secret coves and caves far below were favourite basking sites for Atlantic grey seals. But on this damp autumn morning, the kind her Scottish father would have described as 'dreight', it all looked very different.

She picked her way along the rough

track, stopping to watch the black crows, or were they ravens? She could never tell which was which. Her neck cricked as she gazed up, smiling as they squabbled for the best vantage points on the high brick stack.

The bleakness of the place made her shudder and she wondered again why Lawrence had chosen it. The wind whipped long strands of dark hair across her eyes and she pushed them back, hooking them behind her ear. She stopped to listen. It was easy to imagine the tappings of miners, long since gone, echoing along the labyrinth of the shafts and tunnels beneath her feet.

She'd been watching for the old Land Rover and looked up when she saw it bouncing along the rough track. It was being followed by another vehicle she didn't recognise. Lawrence waved as he drove past, and his two passengers gave friendly nods as the little convoy reached the parking area and pulled alongside Loveday's car.

They all scrambled out, laden with an assortment of bags, painting easels and sketchpads. Released from the captivity of the vehicle, Flossie, whose one brown and one blue eye endeared her to everyone, bounded across the grass to lavish a frantic welcome on Loveday. She laughed, ruffling the dog's neck and feeling a handful of silky fur between her fingers. 'Oh, I know Flossie . . . And I love you too,' she said, screwing up her face to receive the slap of a wet pink tongue.

'Sorry, Loveday,' Lawrence grimaced, striding towards her, 'I'll get around to training her, one day.'

His jeans were threadbare about the knees and he wore his usual shabby safari-style jacket over what appeared to be a clean blue checked shirt. But it was a very different image from the previous evening when he'd made a special effort to dress smartly for his exhibition. He'd been the centre of attention then, with praise lavished on him from all directions. But Loveday sensed something was not right. She'd known Lawrence Kemp for a year and although they were not romantically involved, they were good friends, hence the invitation to be his special guest at the event.

She studied him as he turned to

introduce his little art group, and decided he looked tired.

His eyes narrowed against the sharp wind. 'Meet Jacob and Netta Vincent, from Manchester,' he said.

Loveday held out her hand and the man, short and stocky with a complexion the colour of ripe rhubarb, grasped it in a pumping action. 'You'll be the journalist lady. Just you say where you would like to photograph us.' He nodded across to Netta. 'You'll find the wife and I will be very accommodating.'

Loveday shot Lawrence a glance, but managed to keep a straight face. His wife coloured and offered her hand before scowling at her husband.

The younger of the two women who had driven up in the second car came forward. 'I'm Abbie Grainger,' she said. 'And this is my friend, Kit Armitage.'

They all shook hands, and as Lawrence took his students aside for a briefing, Loveday moved away to take some casual shots. She studied the group from a distance. It was difficult to imagine the two women as close friends. They seemed like complete opposites. Abbie was tall, with long black hair and a tan that Loveday suspected had come from a bottle. She wore an expensive grey fleece over white T-shirt and jeans.

Kit's bright pink anorak looked too flimsy to keep the chill of the wild Cornish cliffs at bay. Her pale hair had been scraped back into a ponytail that pulled her skin so tightly it gave her a startled expression. She lacked her companion's robust, healthy appearance.

The group had circled around Lawrence, listening to his instructions for the morning's painting session, when his head suddenly jerked up. 'Did you hear that?' Everybody stopped talking and strained to listen.

'It's only the wind,' Abbie Fielding said.

'No, there's something else,' Lawrence insisted.

Loveday looked round for Flossie. A few minutes ago the dog had been nosing around the bumps and bushes, her feathery plume of a tail waving excitedly when she'd sniffed out something that might be a rabbit burrow.

Then the sound came again, and this time they all heard it . . . a definite whine.

Lawrence cursed. 'It's Flossie. She's got herself stuck somewhere.'

Jacob clicked his tongue, eager to get on with the business of painting. 'I thought she was a sheep dog. Aren't they supposed to be smart?'

His remark earned him a poke in the ribs from his wife.

'I'm sorry folks. I'll have to look for her,' Lawrence said, taking off in the direction of the whine.

'I'm coming with you,' Loveday shouted, running to keep up with his long stride. They followed the winding path down to the cliff edge. The cliffs here were high and Loveday's fingers were crossed that Flossie hadn't gone over and landed on some inaccessible ledge. Then there were the mineshafts . . . if she had tumbled down one of these then any rescue might be out of the question.

But neither of these things had happened to Flossie. They found her crouched by the cliff edge, whimpering. Lawrence scampered over a rocky outcrop to reach her and as he bent to pick her up, the cove below came into view. He pulled back, his face ashen.

'Stay back, Loveday!'

His hand went out to stop her going to the edge, but it was too late. She was already there and peering down. Someone was on the beach, the white body rigid and motionless. He was lying at a curious angle, arms and legs stretched out in different directions. Then she froze, the bile rising in her throat as she realised she was staring down at a dead body!

Hardly aware of what she was doing, her hand sought out the camera and she began clicking.

'Oh my God,' the voice behind them cried, and they turned to see that the others had followed. Netta's hand was covering her mouth. 'It's a body, isn't it . . . ? There's a dead body down there.'

Loveday raised her arm, warning the woman not to advance further. No one noticed that Kit Armitage, who had been standing behind Netta, had begun to sway, but they heard the thud as she fell and they all rushed to help. Lawrence and

Jacob managed to get her to her feet and supported her between them as they walked her back to Abbie's car. Loveday hurried after them, punching three nines into her mobile phone as she went. All around her voices were raised in confusion. When she got a response she shouted over the mêlée. 'Police please! We need the police!'

Abbie ran ahead and opened the car's back door so Kit, conscious now, but still deathly pale, could be lowered gently inside. 'She'll be fine now. I'll look after her,' she said.

'Well we can't leave her like this. She needs to see a doctor,' Loveday was rummaging in her bag for the unopened bottle of water. She unscrewed the cap and offered it to Kit, who was now struggling to sit up.

'I'm fine, really I am,' she protested. 'I don't know what came over me.' She sipped at the water then offered the bottle back. But Loveday smiled. 'No, you keep it.'

'She's not ill,' said Abbie. 'Kit's grieving.' She gave her friend an understanding smile. 'Her sister, Margaret, died two weeks ago.' She broke off and looked out across the cliffs to where Lawrence was striding back with the Vincents. ' . . . And now this — '

'I'm so sorry,' Loveday said, 'That must have been terrible for you down there.'

Kit began to sniffle and Abbie produced a tissue from her bag as she said, 'I think I'll get her back to the hotel.'

'I think we should all wait here for the police,' Loveday said.

They both stared at her. 'But we don't know anything about this. We never even looked down the cliffs,' Abbie said.

'It's my first time in a situation like this, too,' Loveday said gently, 'But whoever that is down there, he didn't get there by himself.'

'You mean he was murdered?' Kit said numbly.

Loveday nodded. 'Maybe. At any rate, I think we should all stick around until the police arrive.'

* * *

'Sorry, boss,' Detective Constable Amanda Fox spoke into her mobile phone as she pushed open the back door of the Truro police station and headed for her car. 'But something's come up.' She grimaced, anticipating Sam Kitto's reaction at the other end of the line. 'I told the Super that it was your weekend off . . . but he insisted on my calling you.'

Detective Inspector Sam Kitto, of the Devon and Cornwall Constabulary, glanced at the fishing rod propped up against the back door and a taunting image of the river bank, where he'd planned to spend the day, flashed through his mind. He ran a hand through his springy dark brown hair and sighed. 'OK, Amanda. What is it this time?'

'It's a body, boss . . . out at Borlase Cove.'

Sam frowned. Bodies washing ashore were not exactly uncommon in a county bounded on three sides by the sea. They usually turned out to be suicides, or some ill-fated foreign crewman lost overboard from a passing ship. He searched his mind, but couldn't recall any recent reports of missing people.

'What's so special about this one?'

'It looks suspicious, boss.'

'Suspicious?'

Amanda had reached her car and was clicking to unlock the doors. 'It looks like he was tied down to the beach. Sergeant Tregellis and DC Rowe are already there. Want me to pick you up, boss?'

Visions of a recent journey in the passenger seat of his young detective constable's car as she sped along the busy A30, negotiating traffic like an obstacle race, flashed into his mind.

'It's fine,' he said. 'I'll meet you there.' From his cottage in Stithians he'd have a head start on his DC, assuming she was speaking from the station in Truro.

Blue and white incident tape fluttered across the road as Sam approached, grimacing at the valiant efforts of two zealous young officers to preserve a possible crime scene. Several police vehicles, and various other unmarked cars, were already in the parking area. As he pulled alongside them, he spotted Amanda's car speeding over the bumps behind him. He waited for her to park and get out and they walked together across the springy turf, making for the trodden path that wound its way to the figures grouped about the cliff edge.

'What do we know?' he called over his shoulder, as they moved in single file past warning notices highlighting the dangers of underground shafts and tunnels.

'It's weird, this one.' Her voice reached him in snatches as she shouted over the wind. ' . . . Looks like he was tied down to the shingle . . . and just left to drown.'

'He?'

'Seems so.'

Tregellis and Rowe were already taking witness statements. He narrowed his eyes and scanned the horizon. Another sheet of rain was making its way ashore. Sam and Amanda moved to the edge and looked down into the cove. The familiar rotund shape of Home Office pathologist, Dr Robert Bartholomew, clad in the necessary police issue white overalls, was crouched by the body. Two similarly dressed Scene-of-Crime Officers were on their knees amongst the shingle, collecting whatever scraps of evidence were around. Sam was holding out little hope for that. The police photographer was pacing the cove, recording the scene from every angle.

Sam instructed Amanda to take over from Sergeant Tregellis. Will joined him on the cliff edge, following his boss's gaze out to sea.

'Not a lot they can do down there, boss. Doc reckons the tide's been over him a couple of times already.'

'How did the team get down there?'

Will Tregellis nodded towards a lifeboat and two larger fishing vessels that were waiting just offshore ready to offer what help they could. 'The RNLI's inshore boat,' he said. 'It's just about the only vessel that could get into that cove. They're waiting to recover the body and bring the others ashore.'

'Where will they land?' Sam asked.

'There's a beach of sorts just along the coast. We have vehicles waiting there.'

Sam was noting the speed of the waves. 'How long have they got down there?'

'We think about fifteen minutes . . . ten to be on the safe side, before the tide — .'

'I don't think we should hang about for another ten minutes. Let's get these people out of there now,' Sam said.

'But what if they haven't finished?'

Sam's eyebrows descended into a frown. 'Now, Will,' he growled.

Lawrence had joined Loveday, watching the latest arrivals. The woman, in a well-cut dark suit and green wellies, was a good six inches shorter than her male companion. She'd made an attempt to tame her mass of crinkly auburn hair by securing it with a butterfly clip at the back of her head, but the wind was tearing at it, giving her a dishevelled appearance.

The man had a definite air of authority, despite the casual tweed jacket and dark, open necked shirt. He'd glanced briefly in their direction as he passed but showed no inclination to speak to them. Loveday studied him, guessing he was in his mid to late thirties, at least six feet tall, with strong, wide shoulders. His dark hair was brushed back, revealing a high forehead. Even from this distance she could tell his eyes were dark. Not bad looking, she thought, if you liked that serious, rugged type.

He suddenly glanced up and met her eyes. Had that been the trace of a smile? She didn't wait to find out, turning away, embarrassed at having been caught staring at him. It was the woman officer who came over. The other young detective was still having his ear bent by the Vincents.

'DC Fox.' She introduced herself. It was a West Country accent, but not Cornish. She fixed Lawrence with a look. 'And you are — ?'

Lawrence gave his details and described how they found the body. DC Fox jotted the information into her notebook and turned to face Loveday. 'And you — ?' she asked.

The woman's apparent inability to finish a sentence was beginning to irritate Loveday. She smiled at the unreceptive face. 'I'm Loveday Ross,' she said. ' . . . A journalist.' The information had the desired effect and Loveday had to stifle a victorious grin as she watched the woman's bored expression change to one of suspicion.

DC Fox looked up from her scribbling. Loveday had her full attention now. 'Can I ask why you're here, Miss Ross?'

Already feeling guilty at her blatant attempt to antagonise the woman, Loveday smiled. 'Don't worry. It's not a newspaper. I work for a local magazine — *Cornish Folk*.' She had allowed her voice to rise questioningly at the end of the sentence, but the woman gave no indication she had ever heard of the magazine, which was strange considering it was in every newsagents' shop in the county.

'Stop hiding your light under a bushel, Loveday,' Lawrence cut in. 'Loveday's the editor of *Cornish Folk*.'

Loveday frowned at Lawrence's well-meaning attempt to establish her professional status. 'Assistant editor, actually' she corrected. 'And I'm here today because we will be running a feature about Lawrence's art school in the next issue.'

DC Fox clipped the cap back on her pen and Loveday thought she had glimpsed the trace of a smirk. 'You might have to postpone that,' the detective said.

Loveday watched Amanda Fox retreat

in search of the Vincents who had been standing apart, totally engrossed in the activities around them. Until now, she hadn't given a thought to the problems this would cause at the magazine when they no longer had Lawrence's vital article to fill those two empty pages. But as soon as the realisation dawned, Loveday chastised herself. How could she be so callous? What did a magazine article matter when a man lay dead only a hundred feet below? He'd have a family somewhere . . . parents . . . a wife . . . perhaps children. Nobody deserved to be staked out like a trapped animal, waiting to die. The thought made her shiver.

Sam had been keeping an eye on his DC's progress with the witnesses. He liked to stand back like this, watch people's body language. It often told more about a witness than what they actually said. And the body language he had witnessed between the two women just now had been interesting. Amanda had riled the other one. He'd seen the same thing so many times before. The young detective's abrasive attitude put people's backs up. Despite the macabre scene below, he had to smile. He could tell by the way Amanda's back straightened, her shoulders stiffened, and her chin came up, that she had met her match.

He turned to Will. 'Just these four witnesses?'

'No,' Will said. 'There's another couple of women over there.' He flicked a thumb in the direction of the car park. 'One of them felt queasy so they asked if they could stay in their car.' He looked up to catch the attention of one of the uniformed officers. 'I'll get them down here now, boss.'

Sam shook his head. 'Don't bother. I take it you've got their statements?'

'We have. They're visitors, staying along the road at the pub in Polmarth. They've been asked to hang on another day or so just in case we need to speak to them again. The couple over there . . . ' he nodded towards the Vincents, now deep in conversation with DC Fox. 'They're visitors as well . . . staying in the same place as the women.'

'And the other two?'

'Both local. The man's an artist, Lawrence Kemp. Runs an art school locally. The others are his students — oh, all except her.' he nodded towards Loveday. 'She's a journalist.'

Sam's brows knitted together. 'That's all we needed. What's she doing here?'

Will shrugged. 'Some kind of magazine article, I think. It was DC Rowe who spoke to her.'

Below them the lifeboat had moved in to recover the body. Sam knew Dr Bartholomew would accompany it ashore. The crew had already collected the Scene-of-Crime Officers and transferred the group to one of the fishing boats, which was now on its way to deposit them at St Ives harbour.

'I want a word with the pathologist,' Sam said. 'How do I get to the landing site?'

Will gave directions and Sam called over this shoulder as he left. 'Make sure none of the witnesses discuss this with anybody — especially the journalist. What was her name?'

2

A steady drizzle was falling by the time Loveday got back to her cottage in Marazion. The bleakness matched her own mood. The morning's events had upset her more than she'd realised. Dumping her bag on the kitchen table she turned to fill the kettle, but thought better of it and reached into the fridge for the half-full bottle of Chardonnay and poured herself a large glass.

Taking it through to her tiny sitting room, she stood by the window looking out. Through the haze of rain she could just make out the towering mass of St Michael's Mount. She'd noticed while driving along the Penzance seafront that the tide was high. The causeway linking the Mount to the mainland would be well under water. She frowned. The police would have recovered the poor man's body by now.

Her mobile rang. It was Kit Armitage. For a moment she was surprised, then she

31

remembered giving the women her card.

'Loveday? Look, I'm sorry to bother you, but you did say I could call if there was something . . . Well, the thing is . . . I don't suppose you could come over?'

'To Polmarth?'

Loveday could hear another voice in the background. Abbie was giving instructions again.

'There's a pub near here called the Miners' Lamp. Abbie's heard the food is quite good.' She hesitated. 'I don't suppose you would fancy joining us there for a meal?'

'Well . . . er, yes . . . why not,' Loveday said.

'About six then?'

'Fine by me.' Loveday was thoughtful as she clicked off the connection. She hadn't been expecting that and wasn't even sure she wanted to meet up with the women again, but she'd agreed to it now.

* * *

Kit and Abbie had found one of the long tables by the crackling log fire and they were deep in conversation when Loveday walked in. They didn't notice her at first and she took the opportunity to study them. Something about their demeanour suggested a disagreement. The last thing she wanted was to walk in on a row. But the smile Abbie flashed when she looked up made her doubt that first impression.

'We got the best seats in the house,' she called, waving Loveday over.

'So you have,' she grinned, throwing her bag down on the bench.

Kit still had that haunted look, but then she was still grieving her sister.

Loveday had already decided not to talk about the day's events, guessing Kit needed to distance herself from them . . . they all did. But Abbie had other ideas.

'Shame about your little article,' she said.

Loveday raised a questioning eyebrow.

'Well, you can hardly write about it now, can you?'

'It's only been postponed. It *will* be used . . . eventually.'

'Without any mention of the body on the beach?'

'Well of course I won't be mentioning that. *Cornish Folk* is not that kind of magazine.' Loveday looked from one to the other. Was it her imagination or had both women visibly relaxed?

Into the awkward silence, Kit said, 'I made such a fuss today. I feel so embarrassed about it now. I mean . . . fainting. I've never done that before.'

She attempted a weak smile.

'Can't be easy getting over a shock like that . . . not on top of everything else,' Loveday said quietly.

'That's really why we asked you to join us,' Abbie cut in. 'Thanks by the way for coming. You were so kind back there. We just wanted to thank you properly. So the meal is on us.'

'It's very generous, but you really don't have to — '

But Abbie was holding up a hand. 'We insist.'

Menus were produced and they made their choices. Abbie asked for the wine list and ran her eye down it.

'Hmm, I'm impressed,' she said, ordering a South African Sauvignon Blanc.

It was cold and delicious, and Loveday made a mental note to look for it next time she was in the supermarket. 'I suppose you'll be heading back to London now?'

Abbie swirled the wine her glass. 'Actually, no. The police . . . ' She paused, a glint of mischief in her eyes. 'The big, handsome one wants us to hang around for a few days.' She glanced across at Kit. ' . . . And that's fine by us. Cornwall without the tourists . . . what could be better?'

Loveday felt her shoulders stiffen. She knew exactly who Abbie meant, and for some reason her reference to the senior detective annoyed her. She forced a smile as she changed the subject. 'I take it you know this area.'

Abbie shook her head. 'Er, no . . . not at all. Kit and I just appreciate how lovely and quiet it is here at the moment. Besides,' She lifted her glass and took another sip. 'Lawrence has been absolutely wonderful. He's arranged to take the Vincents and us to St Ives tomorrow to paint down at the harbour. I think it's his way of trying to cheer us all up.'

'He's a nice man,' Loveday murmured. 'I'm sure you'll all have a wonderful time.'

'Will you be there?' Kit asked.

Loveday shook her head. 'Sorry, I can't manage that. But I do still want to interview everyone for my article. Maybe in a few days we could meet up for a chat?' She saw the look that passed between the women and quickly added, 'You know the sort thing, how you found the painting experience, what you got out of it.'

'A lot more than we expected,' Kit said gloomily.

'Yes, it's really spoiled things for you,' she sympathised.

'They were spoiled before this morning,' Kit said flatly.

The woman looked so despondent that Loveday wanted to go round the table and hug her. 'I'm sorry, I didn't mean to rake all this up again.'

Kit smiled. 'It's not your fault, Loveday.' Glancing at Abbie she added. 'And we would love to help with your article.'

Their food arrived and as the mouth-watering aromas reached Loveday she realised she hadn't eaten since breakfast. Conversation was suspended as they tucked in to their supper. Abbie and Loveday ate heartily, but Kit merely moved her food around the plate.

'Not very hungry,' she said apologetically, when she caught Loveday's concerned glance.

Judging by the woman's painfully thin appearance, Loveday wondered exactly what she did eat.

'What are you planning to do while you're here?' she asked.

Abbie swung her glass up and drained the last dregs. 'We haven't decided yet. Perhaps you could recommend something?'

Loveday laughed. 'Well just about everywhere in Cornwall is worth a visit, especially if you're staying on for a bit longer.'

Kit was looking miserable again.

But Abbie appeared in high spirits. 'We have a holiday to enjoy and we're determined to do that.' She looked across at her friend. 'Aren't we, Kit?'

The woman forced a bright smile. 'Of course we are.'

Loveday bit back her annoyance. Why couldn't Abbie see just how miserable her friend was? If she actually *was* a friend, that is. It wasn't how Loveday treated her friends. Kit so obviously just wanted to go home and nurse her grief . . . and who was to say that she shouldn't?

But she squared her shoulders and told them about the spectacular Minnack Theatre, the current exhibitions at the Tate in St Ives, and listed her favourite historic houses. 'How long have you got?' she added, laughing. 'Because those are only a few of the places you could visit. You must take a trip up the River Fal. It's absolutely beautiful — even at this time of year.'

'I love boats,' Abbie's eyes sparkled with what Loveday felt was the first real interest she'd seen in either of the women.

'So you're a sailor?' Loveday asked.

'Heavens, no. I've never set foot on a boat in my life,' she said quickly. 'But I love looking at them . . . all those yachts at anchorage . . . I could sit for hours just

38

watching them come and go, and imagine what exotic places they've visited . . . and where they are sailing off to next.'

The look on Kit's face suggested she did not share her friend's enthusiasm.

Loveday smiled, reaching for her bag.

'You're not going?' Kit said.

'I'm afraid I must. I've enjoyed our chat,' she said, getting up. 'And thanks for my supper.'

'Perhaps we can do it again before we go home?' Abbie suggested.

'Why not? But you must come to the cottage next time. I'll cook for you,' she offered, and immediately regretted the rash invitation.

'Have you heard any more from the police, by the way?' Abbie asked as Loveday turned to go.

'No, but then I wouldn't expect to.'

'I thought they had to keep the press informed of developments in a case like this.'

Loveday frowned. 'No, I told you, not a magazine like *Cornish Folk*. We don't really cover news.'

'But you must be privy to what's going

on . . . I mean, you'll have colleagues on newspapers who would be in the know.' She smiled teasingly at Loveday, 'Don't tell me you don't talk to each other?'

'For heaven's sake, Abbie, stop interrogating her,' Kit turned to Loveday. 'I'm sorry. Abbie gets carried away sometimes.'

There was an awkward silence before Abbie said, 'Kit's right. I'm sorry. It's just that we can't stop thinking about that poor man.'

Loveday had been doing her best to avoid thinking about the horrors of that morning.

'The police really haven't been back to me. If I knew any more about what was going on I would tell you.'

But as she started her car outside the pub, she wondered if that was true.

It was dark when she got back to Marazion. The last thing she expected was to meet another vehicle emerging from her driveway. She braked hard as the driver of the old silver Lexus lowered his window and indicated for Loveday to do the same.

'This is a bit of luck,' said Detective

Inspector Sam Kitto. 'I wanted a word with you, but your neighbour . . . Mrs Trevellick . . . told me you'd gone out for the evening.'

It was the first time she'd heard his voice and the rich Cornish burr sparked a strange fluttering in her chest. His eyes were just as dark as she had initially thought — a deep, melting brown. And right at that moment they were fixed intently on hers.

She opened her mouth to speak, but Sam was there first. 'Look, I'll turn further along the seafront and come back. Can we have a chat?'

The last thing she wanted was to go over the day's events again. But maybe telling them to those deep brown eyes might not be so bad.

She lifted her chin. Whatever odd things were happening to her insides, she had no intention of letting him know about it. 'Well you seem to have tracked me down, inspector,' she said coolly. 'Although, isn't this a bit late in the evening for interviews?'

'This isn't an interview, Miss Ross, it's

just a chat. I won't keep you any longer than necessary . . . I promise.' He was studying her, and she was glad it was dark for annoyingly, her cheeks suddenly felt hot.

'Would you like a drink?' she asked, turning to the fridge after he followed her through the back door and into the kitchen.

He eyed the wine bottle she was opening and reluctantly shook his head. 'I expect you'll have been going over in your mind what happened this morning.'

'I've been trying *not* to think about it,' Loveday said.

Sam nodded. 'Understandable. But sometimes things come back — little things that maybe you didn't consider worth mentioning first time.' He raised his shoulders. 'Something you might not even have thought of before.'

'I've already told your officers everything I can remember.'

'What about when you first arrived on the clifftop, Miss Ross, before the others came. Did you see anyone else . . . someone out walking maybe?'

Loveday wished he would stop calling her Miss Ross. She tried to think, but there had been no one else at Borlase that morning . . . or if there was then she hadn't seen them.

Sam nodded, 'OK. So how long had you been there before the others turned up?'

She shrugged. 'About half an hour I suppose.' She saw his eyebrow arch slightly and rushed on defensively. 'I wanted to get there early . . . to do a recce.'

'A recce?'

'Yes, check out the area . . . select the best sites for the pictures, that kind of thing.'

'Of course,' he said. 'You're a journalist.'

He'd said the word as though he'd only just remembered. But he didn't fool her. She knew he would have made it his business to know exactly who she was. She wasn't sure she liked his little deception . . . but he was a policeman, and as he said, this was a murder inquiry.

'Did you go anywhere near the cliff edge?'

'No . . . well, not until we went looking for Flossie.'

'Flossie?'

'Lawrence's dog.'

Loveday frowned. 'Excuse me, Inspector, but why are you even asking this? Surely whoever killed that poor man got to the cove by boat.'

'Why would you assume that?' Sam had a way of looking at her that made her blood course faster.

She stammered. ' . . . The cliffs . . . well they're not exactly climber friendly.'

'Could Lawrence climb them?'

She looked up sharply. Why was he asking that? 'Maybe . . . ' she hesitated. ' . . . But not with a body in tow.'

'Who says there would have been a body in tow? Our victim could have climbed down with his killer, and then been attacked on the beach.'

Loveday sat up. She didn't like the way this conversation was going. 'You're not suggesting Lawrence had anything to do with this?'

'Why did he choose the cliffs for that morning's art class?'

44

She shrugged. 'You'll have to ask him that, inspector.'

Until now Loveday hadn't given much thought as to how the body might have got there. She'd been trying to avoid remembering that image on the beach. But now that they were having this conversation, she was sticking to her guns.

'I still think your killer came in on the tide, which rules Lawrence out because I know for sure that he doesn't know how to handle a boat.'

'He might not have needed to be a great sailor . . . not if he knew that bit of coast really well.'

Loveday stood up, glaring down at him. She was annoyed now that he was still wearing the tweed jacket that had reminded her of her father. 'Is this the only line of enquiry you're pursuing?'

'I think you know, Miss Ross,' he replied lightly, also getting to his feet, 'that I can't discuss that.'

He was treating her like an intrusive journalist and Loveday felt herself bristle. Was he enjoying making her angry?

He was heading for the door, his big frame making the small room feel even smaller. 'I've appreciated our chat . . . and we *will* be considering everything you've said. And oh, just one more thing.' He turned to face her. 'Did you actually take any photographs today, Miss Ross?'

The question took Loveday by surprise. She'd forgotten about the pictures. An uneasy chill was beginning to sweep through her as she recalled that moment at the edge of the cliff when she lifted her camera and began clicking. Should she have mentioned this when she was questioned earlier? She looked up, holding his questioning stare, and nodded. 'But I don't think they'll help much. They're still in my camera. I haven't even looked at them yet.'

He was looking at her, in a way that said what kind of journalist wouldn't have checked out the pictures.

'Perhaps I could see them?'

Loveday inclined her head. 'The police headquarters is only a few minutes from my office in Truro, and I have to go in tomorrow. I'll bring the camera along in the morning. You can download the pictures.' There was no way she was handing over her camera. It had nothing to do with this investigation.

'That will be fine,' Sam said, turning to go.

She winced as he bumped his head on the low lintel over the front door, but she didn't apologise for not warning him about it.

3

The raucous cries of the gulls on the roof of Loveday's cottage woke her next morning, or maybe it had been the sun streaming in through the gap in the curtains. She got up and threw open the window. Out in the bay a solitary yacht, its white sails billowing, glided in front of the Mount. The wild rabbits that lived beneath the hedge round her garden were up and about, breakfasting on the thick grass below her window. The phone rang as she was stepping out of the shower. It was Merrick Tremayne, the magazine's owner, and Loveday's boss. She cursed under her breath. She should have called him. He'd have heard about yesterday's drama and would now be panicking about those two blank pages that still had to be filled. But she was wrong. His voice was full of concern.

'You should have rung me. I've been worried . . . well, we all have. What a terrible thing finding a body like that.'

'Hang on, Merrick. How did you know about that?'

'Sam Kitto rang me. Don't even think about coming in this morning.'

'Inspector Kitto? You know him?' Her voice rose in surprise.

'What? Well, yes of course I do,' he said distractedly, a touch of irritation creeping into his voice. 'Look, Loveday. I really do want you to take the day off. Delayed reaction can be serious.'

'Thanks for the concern.' So Merrick and the inspector were buddies? She wondered what else the policeman had told her boss about her . . . or the other way round, perhaps? She forced her mind back to her work. 'We still have the problem of those two empty pages . . . remember?'

But Merrick waved her protests aside. 'Don't worry. Everything's sorted. We've been digging into the picture files and come up with a good enough collection of photos to make a spread. I'll go in today and write the copy and we'll easily fill that space.' He paused. 'So you see, Loveday,

49

in the nicest possible way, you're just not needed in the office today.'

Merrick was a perfectionist, and although he seldom overruled her in the running of the magazine's editorial, he was quick to step in if he felt something wasn't right. She knew he wouldn't be happy using this emergency stopgap material.

'I *am* fine,' she insisted. 'And I appreciate your concern, but it's my job to fill those pages, and I will.'

'Er . . . excuse me young lady. I'm still the boss around here, and I'm telling you to leave this to me.'

Loveday sighed. From her window she could see the sun glinting on the water. She suddenly had an urge to be out running across the white sandy beach. 'Well . . . if you're sure — ' she said hesitantly.

'Perfectly sure,' Merrick insisted. 'You just relax today. That's an order.'

'Thanks, Merrick. I appreciate this,' she laughed, and knew he was smiling too, as he rang off.

When she put the phone down she was still wondering about Merrick's friendship with the big detective. Twenty minutes

later she was jogging along the beach following the tide line. The air was tangy
and she could taste the salt. A breeze had
sprung up and was creaming the tops of
the waves. A sudden image of the body
in the cove flashed through her mind,
making her shiver. Would she ever get the
horror of it out of her head?

The policeman had asked for her
camera. When she didn't turn up with it
as promised, he'd be suspicious. But what
did she care? There would be nothing of
interest in any of the pictures anyway.
Even so, she was curious now as she
turned and headed for home.

The camera was still in the satchel along
with the rest of her equipment. She pulled
it out and switched on her laptop. As it
whirred into life she extricated the camera's memory card and slid it into the
computer. There were 138 pictures on
the card. She'd forgotten to erase the
ones she'd taken last week. Identifying
the clifftop shots, she put them into a
separate folder and viewed them as a full
screen slide show . . . nothing special
about these. Then she gasped as the shots

she'd taken when she first saw the body flashed across the screen. The man was staked out spread-eagled below. She could even zoom into his face if she chose. Her hand went over her mouth. Sam Kitto mustn't see these. His opinion of journalists was already low enough. She replayed the slide show and squirmed at the very thought that she could have taken such pictures. But it had been a reflex action, her journalist training kicking in. It wasn't as though she ever planned to use them. But she knew the detective might not see it like that. Saving the images into her laptop, Loveday ejected the card and put it back into her camera, and then she deleted the shots of the cove. Sam Kitto wasn't going to see them.

She jumped as someone knocked the front door. Not Cassie; she always came through the kitchen. The young PC who stood there was tall and thin with a round, red face.

'Miss Ross? DI Kitto has asked me to collect a camera.'

Loveday went back to her sitting room and removed the camera's memory card again. 'I think this is what he wants,' she said, sliding it into an envelope.

The constable cleared his throat and Loveday noticed the colour in his cheeks had deepened. 'I believe I have to collect the camera as well,' he said.

Loveday shook her head. 'I don't think so.' She was beginning to feel sorry for the young man. 'I need the camera for work,' she explained, smiling. 'Your inspector will find all he wants here.' She held out the envelope and the constable took it.

The police car was hardly out of the drive when Cassie tapped the back door and walked in. 'You've been holding out on me, girl,' she said.

'Enlighten me,' Loveday said.

'Your dishy policeman . . . Was that him again?'

'That was a very young, still wet behind the ears, PC.'

'Not the one with the come to bed eyes who came last night then?'

Loveday narrowed her eyes, laughing. 'Have you been spying on me?

'How else can I find out things if you don't tell me?'

Loveday shook her head, but she was still smiling as she re-packed her equipment satchel. 'Ok. I'll tell you exactly what happened yesterday.' She made coffee as she described how she and Lawrence had found the body in the cove. Cassie listened, blinking in disbelief as the story unfolded.

'But that's awful. Why didn't you come knocking on my door yesterday?'

'The police asked us not to discuss it with anyone. The only people I've spoken to are the ones who were there when we found the body.'

Cassie pulled out a chair and sat down. 'It was on Radio Cornwall news this morning, but I'd no idea you were involved.'

'Did they name the dead man?'

Cassie shook her head. 'I think they are still trying to identify him. What did the young copper want?'

'The policeman — the dishy one, as you described him, who called last night — wants to look at the pictures I took yesterday.' She was regretting deleting the cove shots now. Could that be construed

54

as withholding evidence? If she was honest, she had no idea why she had done it, apart from this worrying feeling of guilt.

'Is he married?' Cassie had perfected the art of looking innocent when she asked a loaded question.

'Cassie, for heaven's sake! How should I know?'

Cassie tapped her ring finger. 'Don't tell me you didn't notice if he was wearing a ring?'

Loveday grabbed a cushion from a kitchen chair and swiped at her, laughing. She'd absolutely no idea if Sam Kitto was married. She turned so that her friend wouldn't see her mouth twitch. But he was definitely *not* wearing a ring.

'OK, I get the message.' She gave Loveday a good-natured scowl. 'If you're not going into the office, why not come with me to Falmouth Marina. There are a few bits I still need to check over on the Blue Lady. In fact,' she added decisively, 'Come across and have lunch with us.'

Loveday was about to protest when Cassie cut in, 'Oh, don't look like that.

It's just soup and a sandwich.' She tilted her head and grinned. 'Even you can manage a salad sandwich.'

Loveday relented. She liked Cassie and her family. It had been her lucky day when she rented the little cottage in the grounds of Cassie and Adam's big house. Their children were adorable, and Loveday was always secretly flattered when they called her 'Auntie Loveday'.

After lunch Loveday offered to drive them to the marina. 'You're about to get a taste of how the other half lives,' Cassie said, giving directions into the marina's parking area.

'What if your clients are not on board?' Loveday asked, as her friend reached into the back of the car for the black leather case that was her travelling workshop and produced a set of keys.

'They're up north somewhere at the moment,' she explained. 'But they trust me — at least Magdalene does. I don't know the husband, not that it matters because it's Magdalene's boat.'

Loveday looked around. There weren't as many yachts as she'd expected. But

Cassie explained it was getting late into the season and some owners had already started to remove their vessels.

She didn't know much about boats, but the *Blue Lady* was a stunner by any standards. It was white, and sleekly elegant, with three dark blue flashes running from bow to stern. Cassie unlocked the door and the smell of affluence wafted out as Loveday followed her down three steps into what felt like a mahogany palace. Ahead, between two banks of seating, upholstered in a sumptuous blue fabric, was a dining table. Beyond that in the bow of the boat, Loveday could see two double berths in the same luxurious fabric. To her left, a cooker and tiny sink gleamed in the galley, and more berths were visible in the stern. The polished mahogany walls continued behind them, where a small office space with a desk had been fashioned into another corner.

Loveday gazed around her. Every nook and cranny had been utilised. It was a marvel of technology. 'It's amazing,' she said. 'How do they manage to pack away so much in such limited space?'

'Oh it's an art, all right,' said Cassie, 'You should see the business end up top.'

Loveday spun round. 'Have you done all this, Cassie?'

'Just the fabrics . . . and a few other refinements.' She put her case on the table and took out a file and pen. 'The refurb is all but complete. I just need to check that the fitters have done their job and that everything meets with the specifications of the client.'

'Who did you say they are?' Loveday asked, wandering around the cabin for a closer inspection.

'Magdalene Carruthers. She's an interior designer. I think this was a kind of experiment to see if she could break into the yachting market.'

'You mean she's going to pinch your business?'

Cassie laughed and shook her head. 'Magdalene's not interested in working on boats. But people who own expensive yachts also have grand houses, so we can put business each others' way. It works really well, actually, and anyway, Magdalene has pots of money in her own right, she doesn't need to pinch my business.'

'What about Mr Carruthers?'

'I don't know much about the husband, except that his name's not Carruthers. I caught a glimpse of him climbing aboard one day when I was in the car park. He's some kind of legal eagle, I think. They've only recently moved to Cornwall from Cambridge. That's where Magdalene started her business in her maiden name and it just stuck.'

'Carruthers of Cambridge does sound familiar,' Loveday said, racking her brain for the connection.'

'She's the daughter of Judge Henry Carruthers. You remember him? He used to sit on all the big court cases.' She grinned. 'The ones nobody else would touch.'

'That's it,' Loveday said as the penny dropped. 'I remember now. But didn't I read something about him dying?'

'That's right, a few years back. That's where Magdalene's money comes from.'

'I see,' Loveday said, continuing her prowl around the boat. There was a watercolour of the Blue Lady on the wall, and she went to take a closer look. Then gasped when she saw the signature. 'Lawrence painted this?' She asked incredulously, wheeling round to stare at Cassie. 'Did you know about this?'

'Of course,' Cassie said. 'I introduced him to Magdalene.'

Loveday's eyebrow arched.

'She asked if I knew anyone who could paint.' She shrugged. 'I thought of Lawrence.'

Loveday remembered the broody landscapes that had hung on the walls of the St Ives gallery. 'It's not his usual kind of thing,' she said.

Cassie came to stand behind her. 'He's come a long way since the early days, hasn't he?'

'Has he? I don't know much about how he got started, he never talks about it.'

'You're right, he is a bit of a mystery man. I met him when he first moved to Cornwall, about five years ago. In those days he would paint anything people were willing to pay for.'

Loveday gaped at her. This was not the Lawrence she knew.

Cassie was thinking back to the day

she'd spotted the scruffily dressed, bearded man sitting on the beach sketching St Michael's Mount. She'd been surprised at the quality of the drawing and asked if he ever painted boats.

'We got chatting,' she explained. 'He was scratching a living painting the more picturesque pubs and cottages and selling the finished pictures to the owners. We agreed a price for a painting of Adam's boat.' She smiled, remembering, 'It was Adam's birthday present that year.'

'Lawrence has never told me any of this.' Loveday said.

Cassie frowned thoughtfully 'No . . . he's not one for talking about his past, is he?'

Loveday well knew his skilful avoidance of subjects he did not want to discuss — and his life before Cornwall was one of them. She turned back to the painting, and felt an involuntary shudder sweep through her. Why would he keep something as innocent as this a secret?

Inspection over, Cassie began packing her files away, then noticed the slightly open drawer in the office area. She 'tut-tutted'. What had the fitters been doing in that part of the boat? They'd had strict instructions to leave it alone. She got up and slid the drawer closed. It had been empty anyway. The Bentines weren't naïve enough to leave private papers just lying about. After one final check around, Cassie nodded her approval. 'I think we can go, now.'

They went back up the polished steps and, satisfied the Blue Lady was once again locked and secure, walked slowly back along the pontoon to the car.

On the drive home Cassie clicked on the car radio, and they listened in silence to Radio Cornwall's latest news bulletin. The Borlase man, as Loveday had now come to think of him, was the first item.

'Police are still trying to identify the body of a man found in Borlase Cove two days ago. It's understood that the body was partially covered by water when discovered by members of the public on the remote cove. An air sea rescue helicopter from RNAS Culdrose was scrambled to the scene, but it was too late to help the casualty. The body

*was recovered by the St Ives Lifeboat.
The results of a post mortem are
expected later today. A spokesman for
Devon and Cornwall Constabulary said
no further comment could be made at
this stage.'*

For a moment neither of them spoke,
then Cassie said, 'It's a weird way to kill
anybody . . . I mean, staking him out to
drown like that. The poor man must have
gone through agony.'

Loveday shivered. 'Thanks, Cassie, I've
been trying not to think about that.'

'It's how the Cornish used to deal with
folk who betrayed them, you know . . . in
the old days.'

'Come again?'

'You know . . . when all the little fishing
communities were involved in smuggling.
If one of their own shopped them to the
authorities they would take that person
down to a deserted beach and tie them down
to drown.' She glanced up. 'Just like that
poor man.'

'You don't believe that?'

But Cassie nodded. 'Oh, I think it's

true. There's a pub along the coast from here where they say a former landlady met that very fate.' She sighed. 'But enough of that. Why don't you come over this evening, Loveday? Adam and the kids will keep you too busy to brood on all of this.'

'Thanks, Cassie, that's kind of you, but I've already made arrangements with a long, scented soak in the bath.'

At five o'clock Magdalene Carruthers' red sports car swept up the wide gravel drive, coming to a halt at the point where the house came into view. She sat staring at the fluted columns flanking the front door, imagined climbing that short flight of steps, sliding her key into the lock — and shuddered. She still couldn't believe what she and Martin had done. Her hands shook and she steadied them on the steering wheel as she moved the car forward to park at the rear of the building.

Trenmere, the impressive Georgian villa, had been her reward for agreeing to move to Cornwall with Paul eighteen months before. It had been a mistake, of course. Not even the Blue Lady could make up for having to leave her old life behind. The pungent, sickening smell of the lilies hit her as soon as she opened the front door. She hated the austere white blooms. He knew it, which was why he insisted on having them.

'Lilies might not suit you, my love.' She could still hear the sneer in his voice. ' . . . But they suit me just fine. So you'll have to put up with them.'

Magdalene was suddenly back in that church, walking behind her father's coffin, eyes fixed on its mass of creamy white lilies.

She was in the house now and the suffocating fragrance was everywhere. She felt a wave of nausea rise in her throat. Grabbing Paul's flowers, she hurled them through the open front door. The porcelain vase shattered on impact, sending feather-light petals cascading in all directions. She stood back and surveyed the mess — a futile gesture, which she immediately regretted. But everything had changed now. There was no going back.

4

Detective Constable Amanda Fox extricated the pen she had absent-mindedly pushed into her tangle of ginger curls and used it as a pointer to run down the list in front of her. She and Sam had been going through the reports in the tiny room that the Devon and Cornwall Constabulary economically described as his office. The crime scene had yielded nothing apart from the metal tent pegs and twine used to pin down the body. He looked across the desk at her. He liked Amanda's brusque, no nonsense approach to the job. You knew where you stood with people like that, although she did have a tendency to antagonise some witnesses.

An involuntary smile flickered across his face as a picture of her on the cliff top taking Loveday's statement came into his mind. He could see the journalist, a determined tilt to her chin, no doubt giving as good as she got. Maybe, he conceded, Amanda didn't intimidate *everybody*.

'I've been through these at least three times,' she sighed 'and there's nothing.' She held up her hands in defeat.

'There's never *nothing*,' Sam said. 'It's there . . . we just haven't found it yet. What about the journalist woman's pictures?' He resisted referring to her as Loveday, even if it was how he thought of her.

'Completely useless,' Amanda said, not quite able to suppress the satisfaction. 'No sign of any murderer hiding in the bushes.'

She looked up and met her senior officer's cold dark stare, but was saved from any further embarrassment by the appearance of another member of the team, waving the post mortem report on the murder victim.

'At last,' Sam turned, hand outstretched. 'Thanks Alan.'

He scanned the pages and then looked up, frowning, and flipped them across the desk to Amanda. 'Doesn't help much — death by drowning.'

'Well that wasn't rocket science,' she murmured as her eyes ran over the report. 'At least we have an accurate time of death. We can check what the sea conditions were like then. Maybe he got there by boat.'

That was Loveday's theory, and Sam had already decided she was probably right. He pointed a pen at the report. 'Our man died some time on Saturday, between early evening and midnight. Let's double check if anyone saw him that night.'

He saw Amanda glance at the clock and gave her a wry smile. 'Tomorrow will be fine. You can get off home now.'

After she'd gone, he got up and stood by the window. It overlooked the busy main route in and out of the city and, despite the traffic lights at the roundabout below, it was constantly clogged with daytime traffic. But it was almost seven now, and the city was quiet. He toyed with the idea of calling in at the pub. He knew Merrick Tremayne would be there. A pint of his favourite brew was his way of winding down after a working day. Sam liked Merrick and was prepared to set aside his instinctive distrust of journalists to be friends with the man. God knows he had precious few of those.

He sighed and went back to straighten his desk before leaving the office. Once upon a time he looked forward to this part of the day . . . going home to Victoria and his children. He thought they'd been the perfect match, made even stronger when the kids came along. But it hadn't been long before the cracks began to appear in the marriage.

Victoria hated the Force, and the long and often irregular hours he had to spend at work. She refused to accept that his job was such a huge part of Sam's life. Eventually she issued her ultimatum — the job or his family! It wasn't a fair choice, and the stress of it almost tore Sam apart. After that divorce had been inevitable — and if he was being honest with himself, it had been a relief as well. He felt a burden had been lifted from his shoulders. But he did miss the kids. Jack was eleven now, and Maddie, eight. They were growing up so quickly and it wasn't always easy to get through to Plymouth to see them. He wished they were here with him now.

The pencil in his hands snapped and he threw it down with a curse. His morose mood continued as he headed for home, turning right at the Devoran roundabout and along the country road that would take him to Stithians. He drove past the modern bungalows, with their sweeping, sloping lawns, and pulled up in front of his double fronted stone cottage. It was one of two in a terrace in the heart of the village. He sat looking at it, imagining going in, throwing off his jacket, grabbing a beer from the fridge and slumping down in front of the TV. Suddenly the thought appalled him. He restarted the car's engine and turned, driving out of the village.

It was dark as he turned down into Marazion. The entrance to the Trevillicks' place was concealed, but he'd been here before, and knew to watch for the high stone pillars that flanked the entrance to their drive. The cottage was tiny in comparison to the main house, and he pulled alongside Loveday's white Clio. The sounds of squealing children drifted across from the big house and he stopped to listen. Bath time . . . he remembered nights like this. Seemed like a lifetime ago now.

Loveday never closed her sitting room curtains. It was comforting to see the lights of Penzance and Newlyn twinkling across the water. So she had spotted the low sweep of the car's headlights as it swung into the drive, and had the door open before Sam even lifted his hand to knock.

'Inspector . . . we meet again.'

'I've brought your card back,' he said, more gruffly than he had intended.

He could have trusted this to even his most junior recruit. She sighed . . . so there was to be more questioning. She wondered if the rest of the witnesses were receiving the same attention. Perhaps he suspected her . . . or maybe DI Sam Kitto just didn't trust journalists and he was here to warn her not to sell her story to one of the tabloids? Yes, that was probably it, she thought.

She stood back to allow his tall frame to pass and the soft tweed of his jacket brushed against her arm. It immediately reminded her again of the Harris Tweed jacket her father wore for his fishing days. It was his lucky jacket, he'd told them all, laughing, because when he wore it no salmon could resist swallowing his hook.

Loveday had lit the fire when she got in earlier and Sam went straight to it, warming his hands at the flame. The room suddenly looked crowded.

He made no attempt to hand over the card. She'd turned on the lamps and the room was cosy. She caught him glancing at her half-empty glass.

'I'm sorry. Would you like a drink?' She thought of offering him tea or coffee but that would have been childish. 'Only Chardonnay, I'm afraid.' Was that a smile?

'That would be very acceptable,' he said.

Loveday went to the kitchen and returned with the bottle and another glass, which she filled and handed to him before replenishing her own. He was still on his feet and she gestured towards the sofa as she settled into her own chair with her feet tucked under her.

'Nice cottage,' he said, looking around him. 'How long have you been here?'

Her eyes searched the ceiling. 'Three years. I rented the place from Cassie and Adam, next door, when I got the job on the magazine.'

He was on the point of asking why a career woman like her hadn't taken a flat in Truro, but then in these surroundings, and dressed in those jeans and thick white sweater, the career image didn't really suit her. She was watching him, so he sat down, placing his glass carefully on the small table beside him. 'It's not an interview,' he said. 'Sorry if it came across like that.'

Loveday raised an eyebrow and Sam realised she was waiting for some other explanation for his visit. He fumbled in his jacket pocket and produced a small brown envelope. 'Your card,' he said, offering it across.

Loveday reached out to accept it. 'Any use?' she asked.

'We haven't analysed the pictures yet.'

Still the policeman, she thought, and giving away nothing. They sipped their drinks in silence for a few minutes then DI Kitto said, 'It must have been a terrible shock . . . coming across a sight like that.'

He saw Loveday's fingers tighten around her glass. She was back on the cliffs and staring down into . . . horror. She gave a sudden shudder. 'How could anybody be so cruel?'

'You'd be surprised just how nasty some characters can be.'

'I suppose you see this all the time, in your job.'

Sam put down his glass. It had been nine months since his last murder case in Redruth, a drugs-related stabbing. They had caught their culprit the next day. 'Thankfully we don't have too many murders in Cornwall,' he said, his face still grim from the memory of yesterday.

Loveday was thoughtful. 'It's how the Cornish used to deal with those who betrayed them.'

Sam was staring at her and she realised she had spoken her thoughts aloud.

'Come again?' His eyebrow had lifted. He was getting comfortable.

She coloured, feeling foolish that she had spoken her thoughts aloud, but he was still staring at her waiting for an explanation.

'It's just something Cassie told me. There's a pub along the coast where something similar is supposed to have happened years ago.'

She repeated the story as he watched her with growing amusement. She pointed a warning finger. 'Don't you dare say it's an old wives' tale.'

He grinned. 'I would never be so disrespectful . . . ' well, not out loud anyway, he thought.

'So you have a better explanation then as to how this poor man got there,' Loveday said accusingly.

'We're still working on it,' Sam said.

'Do you at least know who he was?' Loveday persisted. 'I mean, was he local?'

Sam's look was non-committal. 'We haven't identified him yet.'

He was the policeman again and Loveday realised her journalist training had unwittingly taken over. She was quizzing him . . . and DI Kitto was giving nothing away.

They sipped their drinks in awkward silence for a few moments before Loveday said, 'You really don't trust journalists, do you inspector?'

His brows knitted. 'You really don't trust policemen, do you Miss Ross?'

Loveday couldn't suppress her grin. She raised her glass. 'Truce?'

Sam did the same. It was the first time she had seen him properly smile and the effect surprised her.

'Have you eaten?' she asked, trying to remember what her fridge had to offer. 'There won't be much, but I could probably manage an omelette and a few bits of salad.'

'No, I'm fine, thanks,' he said abruptly, draining his glass as he stood up to leave.

Loveday shrugged. Apparently an offer to share her supper had been a step out of line and he was putting her in her place by refusing. He really *didn't* like journalists. He went out and she winced as he bumped his head again on the low lintel over the front door. She should have reminded him about that.

'Thanks for bringing the card back,' she called as he slid in behind the wheel of his car. She watched as the red taillights pulled away, and stayed watching as they moved along the drive and out towards the main road.

Sam stopped to pick up fish and chips when he reached his home village. He ate them from the wrapping with a can of cold beer in front of the television — and imagined Loveday enjoying her omelette with another glass of Chardonnay.

★　★　★

Magdalene had been pacing the room, wondering if she dared ring Martin when the pictures of Borlase Cove flickered across the giant flat screen television that Paul had insisted on placing above the fireplace. She cringed every time she saw it. An announcer was reading the local news headlines.

'Police have still not identified the body of a man found in a cove in West

Cornwall on Saturday.'

She stopped, reaching for the remote and turned the sound up. 'The body was discovered by tourists on a painting holiday in the area. Detective Inspector Sam Kitto of Devon and Cornwall Constabulary, who is leading the inquiry, said in a statement that the man was believed to be aged around 40, 5ft 11ins tall and of slight build with thinning ginger hair.'

Magdalene stared at the screen and felt the bile rise in her throat. It was Paul! They had found her husband's body!

Her hand shook as she punched in Martin's number, then immediately cancelled it. Wait, she told herself. Think first! In her mind's eye she could see Paul, as he'd looked last Friday evening, striding across the room towards her. He hadn't expected her to return. She'd forgotten her mobile. His grip tightened round the brandy glass he was holding as he tipped the contents down his throat. He slammed it down on the desk, his face contorted with rage.

'Did you think I didn't know about

your fancy man?' He'd moved forward, and his mouth was twisted into an evil grin. She could feel his breath on her skin. 'I've had you followed . . . Oh yes,' he scowled, 'you didn't know that, did you? Well you and your holy boyfriend — or should I say unholy boyfriend? — You're going to get what's coming to you . . . won't that be a nice little scandal?'

Magdalene's throat tightened. She'd tried to speak, to explain, but no words came.

'Well, what's wrong little girl?' he leered. 'Is Daddy not here to bail you out any more?'

Magdalene moved away from him, but Paul grabbed her arm, 'You didn't really think I was going to let you get away with this . . . did you?'

Her fists tightened and the fear that had initially gripped her suddenly turned to fury. She rounded on him, lifting her chin to match his venom with her own. 'No Paul, not this time! This time *I'm* giving the orders . . . and you'll do nothing.'

He raised his hand and she thought he

was about to strike her, but he stepped back, his face registering disbelief. She took courage from that and pushed him further away. 'It stops here!' she screamed. 'All your evil plots . . . they stop right here!'

But the sneer was back on his face. 'Oh yes?' he taunted. ' . . . And just what do you plan to do about it?'

Suddenly she knew exactly what she was going to do about it. He stared after her as she ran. Her mind was made up. There was no other way!

Reliving the ugly scene had left her drained. She poured herself a gin and drank it down straight, then rang the mobile she had bought Martin for their exclusive use.

His voice, when he answered, was muffled. 'For pity's sake, Mags. We agreed not to call each other. I've had to come out of a meeting.'

Magdalene's temper snapped. 'I'm sorry if this is inconveniencing you, Reverend.' She hated hearing the sarcasm in her voice but was helpless to stop it. 'You haven't heard the news, have you?'

She tried to keep her tone steady but it rose alarmingly on the final word.

'What news?' he snapped. Martin had moved along the corridor of the youth centre where his meeting was taking place.

'It's him! They've found him, Martin.' Her voice wavered and she held the edge of the table to steady her. 'I think they've found Paul's body.'

Hesitantly she recounted the details of the news bulletin.

'Calm down, darling.' Martin tried to speak soothingly. She sounded as if she was falling apart. He had to think fast.

'I'm going to the police,' Magdalene said flatly.

'No! We need to think about this.' He could see his world collapsing. They had done a terrible thing and there would be no forgiveness once it came to light. It had all started so innocently that first day when she came to him. He'd noticed her in church, of course. Who hadn't? A chic, stylish, beautiful young woman stood in his church. But she didn't seem to notice the envious glances of the other female parishioners, or the more meaningful stares of the men in his congregation. That Sunday, as he stood at the door of the church after the service shaking hands with his parishioners as they filed out, she had held his hand just a bit longer than the others. It prompted him to ask if she was all right. She smiled and nodded her thanks, but he noticed that she had lingered in the churchyard until the last people had gone. He waited as she walked back up the path towards him.

'Can I speak to you, vicar?'

In the small room at the back of the church where his robes and the flower vases were stored, he pulled out a chair and invited her to sit. She ignored the chair.

'I don't know where else to turn.'

To his surprise large tears rolled down her cheeks and she looked so vulnerable that he had to stop himself from gathering her into his arms and whispering soothing words. He listened, intrigued, as she poured out the story of a disastrous marriage.

The unexpected interruption of his other mobile made them both jump. His home number flashed and he clicked it on. 'Don't tell me you're going to be late, again, Martin?' His wife, Joan's voice was slightly irritated. He could hear his children in the background — 12-months-old Timmy, Jemima 4, and their six-year-old twins, Sophie and Rory — they were squabbling.

Magdalene was rummaging in her bag for a tissue. 'I'm keeping you,' she said, making for the door. 'Thanks for listening to me.'

Looking down into her large blue eyes he should have recognised the danger signs. She wasn't, after all, the first attractive, vulnerable female he'd had to deal with. It wasn't as though he didn't know the pitfalls. But he heard himself arranging to meet her next day — to talk things over.

It hadn't taken long after that for their relationship to develop into an affair. He hated himself for it. Sitting at the break-fast table each morning, surrounded by the trusting faces of his children as they tucked into their cereal, were the worst times . . . and Joan . . . she didn't deserve this. Why was he risking losing his family? But then he remembered Magdalene, the smell of her skin, the feel of her hair, silky through his fingers. How could he not protect her from the monster she was married to?

This weekend it had all come to a head. Paul Bentine knew about them. He was threatening to destroy him . . . to tell Martin's family about the affair. He couldn't let him do that!

Magdalene's voice on his mobile brought him back to the present.

'I'm going to the police,' she repeated.

His hand shook as he pleaded with her. 'Do you know what you're saying? I'll come over. Don't do anything yet.'

But Magdalene's voice was resolute. 'My mind's made up. I have to tell them.'

5

At 11.30am on Tuesday morning Magdalene walked into Truro Police Station and handed over the photograph of Paul that she had carefully selected from the album. 'I'd like to report my husband missing,' she told the young sergeant. She fancied she noticed his eyebrows rise when he looked at Paul's picture. She gave her name and address, and details of when she had last seen her husband. He jotted them down on a pad then showed Magdalene into a side room. Ten minutes passed before the door opened and a tall man in a dark tweed jacket entered. The woman who followed him was shorter, younger, and with a shock of ginger hair that she had unsuccessfully attempted to tame by tying it back on the nape of her neck.

The man's smile was professional as he extended his hand. 'I'm Detective Inspector Kitto.' He turned to his companion. 'And this is Detective Constable Fox.

Please take a seat Mrs . . . ' He glanced at his notes. ' . . . Mrs Bentine'

She was dressed casually, a suede tan jacket over a light sweater and slacks, but she looked expensive. Sam laid Paul's photo on the table. 'This is your husband?'

Magdalene nodded.

'When did you last see him, Mrs Bentine?'

She shifted in her chair. 'Friday.'

Sam had been watching the woman carefully. He thought she looked more frightened than worried, but there were dark smudges under her eyes that suggested she'd been crying.

'That was four days ago, Mrs Bentine. Why have you left it so long to report him missing?

'I've been away,' she said.

'Until today?'

Magdalene shook her head and her teeth caught her bottom lip. 'I came back yesterday.'

Sam's eyebrows rose. 'Your husband didn't come home last night and you weren't worried? Why not, Mrs Bentine?'

Magdalene shrugged. 'He often stays away. We have what is called . . . an open marriage, inspector.' She looked up, studying him for a reaction, but found none and continued. 'It's not unusual for him not to come home. His business you know. He often stays overnight somewhere without informing me. I told you, we don't live in each other's pockets.'

'But surely you must have wondered where he was?' Amanda asked.

'Paul wouldn't thank me for making a fuss. If I reported him missing and he walked in and found I'd been to the police he . . . well, his reaction would not be pretty.' She put both hands to her face and held her head. 'But you're right. I am worried now. I wouldn't be here otherwise.' She was avoiding eye contact now. Were they believing her?

Sam and Amanda exchanged looks. 'Haven't you heard any local news bulletins?' Sam asked, and saw her body stiffen.

'No'

She was lying . . . but why? Sam drew in his breath and lowered his voice. 'We might have some bad news for you, Mrs Bentine.'

Magdalene kept her gaze fixed on the table. She knew what was coming.

He spoke quietly. 'We've found a body and it matches your husband's description.' He stood up. 'I'm afraid we'll have to ask you to take a look at it?'

Magdalene's legs felt like jelly and she trembled as she stood up. Sam nodded to Amanda to take her to the morgue.

The women stood together behind the glass window as the body was wheeled in, and Paul's dead face was uncovered. Amanda's hand flew to her mouth and she nodded.

'Is this your husband, Mrs Bentine?'

'That's Paul,' she whispered, as her legs gave way and she collapsed into Amanda's arms.

The call to her DI was short and to the point. 'Mrs Bentine has just identified her husband's body, boss, it's Paul Bentine.'

'How is she?' came the sombre response.

'Much as you'd expect, I suppose.'

Sam nodded at the phone. 'I've got her address. We'll meet you up there.'

The grandeur of the Bentine's villa took Amanda by surprise as she followed Magdalene's instructions and parked at the front steps.

'I'm really fine now, DC Fox. There's no need for you to stay.'

'Well, it's not that simple,' said Amanda, following her into the high-ceilinged hall, and trying not to gasp at the sweeping staircase . . . the paintings. 'You haven't asked how your husband died? Aren't you curious?'

Magdalene pivoted round on her heel. 'You said he drowned.' Her voice was accusing.

'We said his body was found in a cove.' Amanda studied the woman's face. The colour had returned and she was being more assertive. 'I'm afraid there's more to it than that.'

'Suicide?' Magdalene said, her eyes full of horror. 'You mean he committed suicide?'

Amanda pursed her lips, took Magdalene's arm and walked with her into the opulent sitting room. 'You'd better sit down,' she said, leading Magdalene to a cream leather sofa and waiting until she was seated. 'We're still trying to establish the facts,' she said quietly.

The woman began to shake violently and the young detective scanned the room for a drinks' tray. She found one on a side table and poured a measure of brandy, then made Magdalene sip it. Her mobile trilled and she answered it. 'Boss?'

'We'll be searching the house. Is she up to it?'

Amanda glanced down at Magdalene. The brandy was taking effect. Some colour had seeped back to the woman's cheeks. 'I think so,' she said.

Sam and Will arrived ahead of the Scene-of-Crimes team. The search of the house was quick, but thorough. They concentrated on the office, asking permission to take both computers and a batch of memory sticks for further investigation.

Magdalene suddenly met Sam's gaze, her large blue eyes now candid. 'He killed himself, didn't he?'

The three officers exchanged glances.

Magdalene persisted. 'I can see by your faces that he did . . . he couldn't swim, you see . . . had a fear of water . . . ' her voice drifted off.

Sam cleared his throat. 'What makes you think your husband killed himself?'

She shrugged; it was a helpless kind of gesture. 'You mean it was an accident?'

'What made you think he'd killed himself?' Amanda had taken over the questions after a nod from Sam. 'Was he depressed?'

'Who knows,' Magdalene said flatly, 'Paul wasn't like other men. If he was depressed he never showed it. Had to keep up the image, you see; keep the clients happy — or they don't pay up.'

'What kind of image, Mrs Bentine?' Will cut in.

Magdalene frowned, as though she had to rack her brain for an explanation. 'Paul is a solicitor . . . was a solicitor.' She produced the ball of hankie and pressed it to her nose while the others waited for her to continue. 'He had a practise in Cambridge. She reached for the teacup and began sipping from it, apparently unaware, or not caring, that it had grown cold.

'My father was Judge Henry Carruthers,' a faint smile touched her lips and she looked around the three faces for any sign that the name would be familiar to them. Amanda nodded encouragingly and Magdalene went on. 'He was very well respected in Cambridge . . . everywhere, really . . . a bit of an icon of the legal world. Anyway, he took Paul under his wing . . . put in a good word in the right places.' She paused, staring into the room again, apparently at memories of another life in Cambridge. 'We were happy then.'

'Why did you come to Cornwall?' Sam asked

Magdalene sighed, 'It was Paul's idea. I still can't understand why we had to move. We were settled in Cambridge. Admittedly his practise wasn't doing particularly well, but I'd set up an interior design business and things were really working for me.' She shrugged. 'But Paul decided it was time for us to leave . . . come to Cornwall . . . enjoy the fruits of his labour, he said.'

'What did you feel about that?' Sam asked.

Magdalene shrugged again. 'My father had died by then, but I still had all my friends in Cambridge, people I'd grown up with. I didn't want to leave. Our marriage had been going through a sticky patch. Paul was always edgy, there were rows, his business was causing him problems but he would never tell me what they were. Anyway, he came up with this idea about moving to Cornwall . . . a new start, he said.' She looked round the room. 'I had to give our marriage that chance, didn't I?'

'And did it work?' Amanda's question took Magdalene by surprise.

'Of course it didn't. In fact, things were a lot worse between us after we came here. Paul had planned to retire, but then he decided that he needed to work after all. He took on a few consultancies with some of the big companies around here, but he was never what you could call happy.

'My business, on the other hand really took off. A lot of my old friends in Cambridge had connections here . . . you know, holiday properties . . . yachts

. . . things like that. And they were more than happy to recommend my services as an interior designer to their friends down here.'

She put the cup she had been nursing carefully back on its saucer. 'Paul didn't like that, of course. He didn't want me keeping up with my old friends, said we needed to make a complete break. But I knew he was jealous. My business was a success, you see . . . and his wasn't.'

The picture she painted was not one of domestic bliss. Sam went to the window. He could see the gravel drive sweep down to the road. There wasn't much traffic in an area like this. 'Your husband did not kill himself, Mrs Bentine,' he said quietly, before turning to face her. 'He was murdered.'

The word seemed to drain away what little colour remained in Magdalene Bentine's face. She attempted to stand, but swayed and Amanda rushed to guide her back down to the sofa. She stared at Sam. 'You think someone killed Paul?' Her voice was incredulous.

'Is that such a surprise?' Sam asked.

'From the way you have described him, your husband seems quite capable of upsetting people.'

'I know he had enemies,' Magdalene said, 'But things were better for him after we moved here.'

'What enemies did he have, Mrs Bentine?' Sam asked.

But Magdalene shook her head. 'I don't know. Maybe enemies is too strong a word. Paul didn't exactly get on with everybody.'

He was certain she was hiding something, but now wasn't the time to press her further. They would interview her again.

'Just one more thing,' he said, smiling as he turned to leave. 'You said you were away for the weekend. Where did you go?'

Magdalene coloured. 'I was staying with friends in Bodmin,'

Sam knew she was lying, but his expression remained the same. 'It's just a formality, but we will need the address of your friends.'

Back at headquarters the computers had been examined at length. The smaller laptop was obviously the one Magdalene used for her business. Nothing of significance had been found in either.

Sam was more hopeful of gaining information from the little memory stick now in front of him. He examined the tiny scrap of purple plastic. It had been dusted for prints and none were found, which was odd because he would at least have expected Paul Bentine's prints to be there. It could be brand new of course, and devoid of any information at all, but he would still have expected to find some prints. This one looked as though it had been wiped.

But the stick was not devoid of information and he'd whistled when they produced the printout of what was found on it. It was a dossier of names. Sam recognised some local businessmen. Each name had an attached file of information — not the sort of details any of them would want to be made public. Bentine was a blackmailer! This morning Sam had no suspects ... now he was spoilt for choice!

The pub was packed with lunchtime

drinkers when Merrick and Loveday walked in.

'Who were those two women desperate to catch your attention back there?' He was referring to Kit and Abbie, who'd been having lunch in a café in the square when they passed. They had knocked the window and beckoned her in, but Loveday shook her head, holding out her hands as though she had another appointment — which she had.

'They looked pretty determined to catch your eye.'

Loveday explained who they were and he nodded. 'I'm not trying to avoid them,' she frowned, 'But they are a bit heavy going — and they seem to appear everywhere I go.'

The man standing at the bar turned as they entered. Loveday's eyebrows rose as they stared at each other, their surprise mutual.

'You two know each other I take it,' Merrick said, slapping Sam's back.

'Miss Ross.' Sam nodded solemnly.

Loveday inclined her head. 'Inspector.'

Merrick eyed them, but said nothing.

He'd let whatever was going on between them pass for now.

'Right,' he said. 'What's everybody having?'

Loveday hated standing at a bar and eyed a corner table by the window. Sam had followed her glance.

'I'll get these,' he said. 'You two sit down and I'll bring the drinks over.'

'How's it going then, Sam?' Merrick asked when the detective had brought their glasses and set them down on the table. 'Got it all tied up yet?' His tone was teasing.

Sam sat down, stretching his long legs under the table as he considered his answer. It would be pointless not telling them, especially as it would be all over the local news by teatime.

They hadn't officially released the dead man's identity, but Merrick was his friend and he trusted him. He wasn't yet sure about Loveday. He lifted his glass and drank down a couple of inches of its contents before wiping his mouth.

'I might as well put you both out of your misery.' He frowned at Merrick, but

Loveday thought she caught a glimpse of humour in his eye, 'Since this is probably why I was invited here in the first place.'

Merrick put down his glass and wiped a foam moustache before widening his eyes. Loveday looked away to hide her amusement at this contrived innocence.

Sam ignored the gesture. He knew Merrick moved in all levels of Cornish society, and seemed to know half the county. He had more to gain by tipping them off now than by letting them wait for the press release.

'The victim's name is Paul Bentine.' Sam watched their expressions for any sign of recognition. 'Does the name ring a bell?'

Loveday shrugged and shook her head, but Merrick frowned. He knew the name . . . but from where? Then he snapped his fingers. 'Got it,' he said. 'Paul Bentine. He's a member of my golf club, or *was* one.' He shook his head and put his half empty glass back on the table. 'Good god,' he said. 'Paul Bentine. I can picture him now, wheeler-dealer kind of bloke, always ducking and diving. Some kind of legal man, not very popular, though.' His mouth twitched into a smile, 'Now his wife . . . she *was* popular; bit of all right, as I remember.'

Loveday frowned at him. She was acutely aware of Sam's eyes on her.

'I didn't mean that,' Merrick said. 'She really was a pretty woman. What was her name now?' He clicked his fingers. 'Magdalene . . . yes, that was it. Magdalene. I liked her. She seemed to be the one with the money. Runs some kind of design business.'

An uneasy feeling was beginning to stir in the pit of Loveday's stomach. She'd heard the name Magdalene already this week. 'You're talking in the past tense, Merrick,' she said. 'Did they give up their membership?'

'I think they were forced to, at least he was. Some kind of scandal. I can't remember much about it.'

He looked at Sam. 'But I can find out if you like.'

Sam nodded his thanks. He'd been watching Loveday, and glanced away, embarrassed when she caught his stare.

He liked the way she'd smiled up at him when he'd brought their drinks.

Would she still be smiling at him, he wondered, when she discovered what he had to do next?

The Borlase murder had made the first item on Spotlight that night as Loveday sat in front of the television picking at a pizza.

'Police have identified the body found at the foot of cliffs at Borlase in West Cornwall on Sunday as prominent local professional man, Paul Bentine.'

She sat forward and turned up the volume. *'Mr Bentine gave up his legal practise in Cambridge two years ago when he and his wife moved to Cornwall. It is understood that Mr Bentine was semi-retired.'*

Her mobile rang and Loveday saw Lawrence's name flash up as she answered the call.

'Loveday?' His normally placid voice was urgent.

'Are you watching Spotlight?'

She told him she was.

'I knew him,' Lawrence blurted out,

'Bentine . . . I knew him.'

Loveday slid her tray onto the coffee table and stood up. 'What do you mean, knew him, Lawrence? What are you talking about?'

' . . . Can I come over?'

She could hear his breathing. It was too fast.

'I need to speak to you.'

She was worried now. 'Of course you can. But tell me what's wrong, Lawrence.'

'When I come over . . . we'll talk then.'

She was still staring at the phone in her hand when there was a knock on the kitchen door.

'Come in Cassie,' she called. Only her landlady used the back door. Cassie rushed past her, face flushed and animated. 'It was him,' she said. ' . . . On the news, it was *him* . . . Paul Bentine!'

'Calm down Cassie and tell me what you're talking about.'

But she had a feeling she already knew. Had all her friends known the dead man? The sinking feeling that had started with Lawrence's call was deepening.

'Paul Bentine,' Cassie gasped. 'It was

his boat we were on at the weekend.'

Loveday sank into a chair. '*He* was Magdalene's husband?'

'Magdalene Carruthers. That's right. She still uses her maiden name professionally. But her husband . . . ' Cassie continued breathlessly, 'I recognised his picture on the news just now . . . it was Paul Bentine.'

After Cassie left, Loveday watched the hands of the wall clock click round. It was almost eleven and there had been no sign of Lawrence. She'd rung his mobile several times but it was going onto his answer phone. She toyed with the idea of going back next door to ask Cassie what she should do, but it was late and she didn't want to waken the children. Deciding there was no more she could do that night, Loveday went to bed.

6

St Ives had been quiet as Sam and Will drove along the seafront. They'd been lucky getting the body identified so soon, and the material they'd found at Bentine's house was a major breakthrough in the case.

He'd been aware of Lawrence Kemp talking to Loveday on the clifftop that morning but he hadn't spoken to him, having left his team to interview the witnesses. The artist's name cropping up on Bentine's blackmail list, however, was too much of a coincidence to ignore.

His place, when they found it, looked like one of the old buildings local fishermen once used as pilchard stores. His accommodation was on the upper floor and reached by a short flight of stone steps. There was no banister and pots of leggy geraniums had been placed on each step. From the landing they could see into a front room. A wood-burning stove stood in front of a bare stone wall. Artists obviously saved their paint for their canvasses.

Lawrence Kemp was as tall as Sam, but skinnier. His sandy hair was thinning at the front but reached below the collar of his black and white check shirt. His jeans were splattered with paint, and frayed at the knees. Sam was never sure if this was a fashion trend, or just ordinary working clothes. In Kemp's case he suspected the latter.

He didn't seem surprised to see them, stepping aside to allow them into the room. It was warm and surprisingly cosy. A battered sofa had been tidied up by the addition of a multi-coloured throw. Table lamps, with shades askew, had been placed at various points around the room. An ancient portable TV sat on low bookcase.

Lawrence indicated the sofa, but Sam crossed the room to lean against a table, arms casually folded. Will, too, remained standing. Kemp did the same, but he appeared to have regained some of his composure and picked up a pouch of tobacco to begin rolling a cigarette. He didn't offer the detectives one.

A painting of some old mine workings hung on the fireplace wall. The moody image dominating the room.

Will Tregellis's eyes had also been drawn to it. 'Where is it?' he asked. 'The mine, I mean.'

Lawrence cleared his throat and tapped the newly made cigarette before holding a match to the end of it. 'Out Land's End way.'

'Looks like the cliffs around Borlase,' Will said.

Lawrence drew deeply on the cigarette and screwed up his eyes against the smoke. 'Why exactly are you here?' he asked.

Sam smiled. 'Just routine,' he said. 'We just need to check a few more things with you.'

Lawrence tapped non-existent ash into a brightly decorated pottery dish by his side.

'You knew Paul Bentine,' Sam said, watching the colour drain from Kemp's face. 'Why didn't you tell us you recognised him down on that beach?'

'Because I didn't,' Lawrence scowled,

looking from one detective to the other. 'For heaven's sake, we were all in shock. We'd just found a body. I didn't climb down to examine the corpse.'

'But you did know Paul Bentine?' Will cut in.

'A long time ago,' Lawrence said quietly.

'Where were you on Friday evening, Mr Kemp?' Sam asked.

Lawrence pursed his lips and looked up at the ceiling. 'Let me see,' he said, 'Friday? Yes, I was here in St Ives.' He looked at each detective in turn. 'You can ask anyone at my exhibition.' He paused to draw on the battered cigarette, feeling pleased at the glance that passed between the detectives. 'There were plenty of witnesses,' he said.

Sam looked up sharply. 'Why do you feel you need witnesses?'

Lawrence's temper flared. 'Look, what's this all about?'

'Paul Bentine, Mr Kemp,' Sam said. 'It's about Paul Bentine. We're trying to find out who killed him. How did you know him?'

Lawrence stubbed out the useless cigarette with force and glared at Sam. 'It's no secret. You can look up your records . . . or whatever it is you do to keep a check on us.'

He watched Sam and Will exchange glances. 'I've been to prison.' He raised an eyebrow. 'Don't tell me you didn't know?' He shook his head and sighed. 'It's all going to come out again. Isn't it?'

'What is?' asked Sam.

'My prison record. It's all going to be dragged up again.'

Sam frowned. 'Not necessarily, but you might as well tell us . . . as you said, we can check. It would just be so much better if it came from you.'

Lawrence Kemp's voice was flat, his eyes haunted. 'I killed three people,' he said.

* * *

Loveday spotted Sam Kitto as soon as she walked into the editorial floor next morning. He was in Merrick's office, together with another detective she recognised from

108

the clifftop that day. All three looked up when she appeared, and Merrick beckoned her in. She shot a questioning glance to her PA, Keri. But Keri shrugged and shook her head.

'I don't know any more than you,' she said in a voice hardly above a whisper. 'They've been in there for about 20 minutes.'

More unease was beginning to surface. Something was definitely wrong. Were they going to tell her Lawrence was dead? She began to shake.

'We won't keep you long, Miss Ross,' Sam said, hoping his professional smile was convincing, but his brown eyes were serious. He indicated a seat.

'I'm fine standing,' Loveday said. 'Is somebody going to tell me what this all about?'

Merrick crossed the room making for the door.

'I would like Mr Tremayne to stay.'

Merrick nodded with a sympathetic smile and returned to his desk.

'Where were you on Friday evening?' Sam asked.

Loveday's eyes widened. 'The night Bentine died? Do I need an alibi now?'

The other detective she'd seen on the clifftop on Saturday, cut in sharply. 'Can you just answer the question, please.'

Loveday ignored him and addressed her answers to Sam. 'I was in St Ives . . . at an art exhibition.' She looked from one to the other and realised they were waiting for her to elaborate on that.

'It was Lawrence's exhibition . . . look, you've got me worried now. Is Lawrence all right? He hasn't been hurt or anything?' Her eyes were searching Sam's face. 'Just tell me!'

'Mr Kemp is fine,' Sam said. 'He's with us at the moment.'

Loveday stared. 'With you . . . you mean at the police station?' She dropped into a chair. 'Whatever for?' She felt more confused than ever now.

'Can you give us a list of everyone who was present at this exhibition?' This from the detective Sam introduced as Detective Sergeant Tregellis.

'Well of course I can't,' Loveday snapped. 'I was only a guest myself. You'll have to ask Mr Kemp. He's the only one I really knew.'

'You can vouch for him being there all evening then?' DS Tregellis asked.

Then she knew. She could feel her anger rising. 'It's not my whereabouts you are checking up on. It's Lawrence's!'

'Just tell us, Loveday,' Sam sighed, not managing to keep the irritation from his voice, 'Was he with you all evening?'

'Never left my side,' Loveday said, meeting his eyes. She hoped he wasn't able to see just how shaken she was. Lawrence couldn't be mixed up in something like this. Could he? Out of the corner of her eye she could see Keri and Mylor Ennis, who designed the graphics for the magazine, casting furtive glances towards the glass partition that separated Merrick's office from the rest of the editorial. They were making a show of getting on with their work, but they were understandably curious.

Keri's brows were knitted. She could tell from Loveday's body language that whatever was going on in Merrick's office, her boss was not enjoying it.

'Did he pick you up from home?' Sam continued.

Loveday shook her head. 'I drove myself.'

'What time did you arrive?' It was DS Tregellis.

'I don't know exactly, probably about seven.'

'And was Mr Kemp there when you arrived?' he pressed.

'It was his exhibition. Where else would he be?' she snapped.

Sam moved towards the door and made an attempt at a smile. 'Thank you,' he said, nodding to Loveday. 'You've been very helpful.' But at the door he turned back. 'Just one more thing. What was Lawrence Kemp wearing?'

'Wearing?' Loveday frowned, trying to remember. 'A dark blue suede jacket, white T-shirt . . . and jeans, I think.'

Why were they asking that? The look that passed between the detectives sent splinters of ice through Loveday's veins. Lawrence *had* been different that night. She knew he'd had something on his mind . . . but not this . . . not murder!

The inspector's voice brought her back into the room. 'Thanks again for your help,' he was saying, adding after a pause, 'We didn't mean to upset you. It's just that we need to ask these questions . . . even if only to rule people out of our investigations.'

Loveday forced a smile. 'I know.'

'Well, if you do think of anything, this is my mobile number.' He thrust a business card into her hand, and she nodded, tucking the card into her pocket.

Loveday suddenly remembered Flossie. 'Who's looking after Lawrence's dog?' she asked.

Sam looked up. 'She's quite safe with a neighbour. Nothing to worry about there.'

Loveday pursed her lips as the detectives left the room and saw they had stopped to talk to Merrick in the main office. Their serious faces did nothing to reassure her. Lawrence was in trouble — and there was nothing she could do about it.

Merrick was smiling reassuringly when he strode back into the office and Loveday said, 'You know Lawrence, don't you, Merrick? He wouldn't be involved in anything like this?'

'I doubt it very much,' he said, putting a fatherly arm around her shoulder and guiding her out of his office 'Why don't you and Keri take an early lunch?'

Loveday pursed her lips. 'You're spoiling me,' she said.

'What else are bosses for?' he grinned.

Keri needed no persuading to join her. 'Danish pastries all round?' she suggested.

Loveday laughed. 'Why not?'

Although it was early, the city's lunchtime buzz was already beginning to stir. A couple of dark-suited businessmen had emerged from one of the smart offices on the other side of Lemon Street and were making their way towards the Lemon Quay piazza. Loveday and Keri were heading for the museum, where the recently opened coffee shop served one of the best cappuccinos in the city.

'Grab a table and I'll get the drinks.' Keri said, nodding to the coveted corner table that was usually occupied by tourists, with their accompanying litter of bags and cameras. Loveday wasn't sure she enjoyed being mothered by Keri, but she felt too drained to complain. She sat down, wondering why the rich smell of the coffee was so comforting. Keri returned with two large cups of frothy cappuccino, generously sprinkled with chocolate, and two cream-filled pastries on a tray. Loveday remembered she hadn't bothered with breakfast that morning, and now, despite herself, she was hungry.

Keri saw her eying the pastries. 'I know,' she grinned impishly. 'They're a car crash, but I couldn't resist them. Anyway,' she added, giving Loveday another of her motherly appraisals, 'you look as though you need a sugar fix.'

Loveday shook her head, but she was laughing.

'That's better,' Keri said, putting the tray on the table and sliding into the chair opposite. 'Now give. What did the police want?'

Loveday recounted her interview with Sam Kitto and his sidekick as Keri listened with growing shock. Her partner, Ben, was an artist and she had met Lawrence Kemp at various exhibitions and art functions. Ben had often described his work as amazing. He was certainly much respected in the St Ives artists' community.

'The thing is,' Loveday said. 'I was trying to contact him last night.' She sat back with a sigh. 'Now I know why he didn't get back to me. He was here in Truro all the time — at the police station. He's probably still there because I tried to ring him while you were at the counter and his phone is still switched off.'

'Why are they questioning him?' Keri wiped sticky crumbs from her mouth.

'That's what I don't know.' Loveday said. 'But I'm going to find out.'

'I don't like the sound of that.' Keri put down her pastry with a scolding look that made Loveday smile.

'I know what you're like, Loveday Ross,' she said, finger wagging. 'You're going to sniff around in places where you're not wanted. It's that journalist thing coming out again. Isn't it?'

Loveday sighed. 'I have to find out what's going on . . . for Lawrence's sake.'

'And what if Lawrence doesn't want you to find out? Maybe this is something private that he doesn't want anybody to know about it. You could stir up a hornet's nest here.'

Loveday dabbed her mouth with the paper serviette that Keri had brought and left the best part of her pastry on her plate. 'I don't think Lawrence would thank me if I did nothing to help him.'

Keri gave her a long look. 'I thought it was strictly platonic between you two?'

'It is . . . believe me. But that doesn't stop me caring about him. I can't turn my back on him, Keri.'

Laura Bennington was the museum's curator, and older than Loveday, but they had become friends since their first meeting almost a year ago when the magazine covered a special geology exhibition. She was now approaching their table looking flustered. Strands of her long ash-coloured hair had escaped from her normally immaculate French pleat and her expression was worried.

'I hoped you two would be in this morning,' she said, lowering her voice and glancing round the room to ensure they could not be overheard, before pulling up a chair and sitting down.

Loveday reached out to touch her friend's wrist. 'Whatever's wrong, Laura?'

'We've been vandalised,' she whispered, leaning closer to speak confidentially. 'Two of our paintings have been spray painted . . . It's awful. I don't know what to do.'

'Have you reported it to the police?' Loveday asked.

But Laura hesitated before shaking her head. 'I don't know what to do. That's why I'm so glad to see you two. If I get the police involved and this is made public . . . well,' she spread her hands in a gesture of helplessness. 'We have some important exhibitions coming. If the organisers think we can't handle security they might change their minds and cancel.'

Her eyes were wide as she looked across at Loveday. 'There's more,' she said, and bit her lip before going on. 'It's Lawrence's paintings that have been damaged!'

Loveday stared at her and then leapt to her feet, her pulse racing. 'Can we see them?'

'Of course. Follow me,' Laura said, hurrying ahead through the maze of ground floor exhibits to the stairs that led to the upper galleries and the art exhibitions.

The local artists' section had been cordoned off with a thick red rope and a sign had been put up that read 'Gallery Temporarily Closed.' Laura unclipped the rope and stood aside to let Loveday and Keri pass. The paintings were displayed on sturdy green partitions, high enough to give the impression that they were fixed walls. They stopped before two paintings that Loveday knew from previous visits were studies of some of the old mine workings around the St Moy area. Lawrence's brooding style was usually instantly recognisable — but not anymore. Both pictures had been almost totally obliterated by angry splashes of red paint. She turned to look around her. None of the other pictures had been touched. The vandal seemed to have targeted just Lawrence's work. Loveday shook her head and gave an involuntary shudder. She could hardly believe what she was seeing. It just felt so violent. Who could hate Lawrence enough to violate his work?

She understood Laura's instinct to

protect the gallery's image, but this was a police matter. Anyone capable of such wanton vandalism might could be capable of . . . well, anything!

'Call the police Laura. You must call them now!' she said.

★　★　★

Cassie was at her kitchen window and gave Loveday a wave as she pulled up by the side of the cottage later that evening. She got out of her car and walked across to the house. The kitchen door opened before she could knock. 'Come in,' Cassie said. 'I'm organised for once and Adam is putting the monsters to bed.'

Adam Trevillick was the town's GP, and Loveday pictured him now, in one of the multi-coloured waistcoats he always wore, sitting on Sophie's bed reading her and her little brother, Leo, their ritual bedtime story.

Cassie looked at her friend with an expression of concern and drew her into the kitchen. 'I've a bottle of wine in the fridge just waiting to be poured. You sit there,' she ordered, pushing Loveday down on one of the chairs at the kitchen table, ' . . . and tell auntie all.'

As they sipped their cold wine, Loveday recounted the day's events and watched Cassie's eyebrow arch higher with each revelation.

'I know Lawrence can't be mixed up in all this, but the police still haven't let him go. I keep thinking of that painting in the Blue Lady and wondering if there's a connection.' She met Cassie's eyes and said solemnly, 'If you know anything, Cassie, you must tell me.'

But Cassie shrugged. 'I don't know any more than you, but I'm going to see Magdalene tomorrow. Maybe she'll know more.'

'Can I come with you?'

Cassie put down her glass and studied her friend. 'What are you up to?'

Back in her cottage Loveday peeled off her jacket and stepped out of her shoes. She had no idea how meeting Magdalene might help Lawrence, but at least she'd be doing something.

She hadn't heard the car arrive so the

knock on her front door took her by surprise. Only strangers came to the front. She opened the door and found a smiling Abbie, bottle of wine in her hand, and the more reticent figure of Kit behind her.

'Just a thank you,' Abbie said, proffering the bottle.

Loveday raised a questioning eyebrow.

'For pointing us in the right direction . . . all those sightseeing ideas,' she went on breathlessly, 'We would never have found all those wonderful places if we had stuck to the tourist trail everybody else follows.'

She forced a smile, standing aside to let them come in. So much for her quiet evening in.

Kit's eyes lit up when she walked into the cosy room 'This is lovely. You're so lucky having a place like this. Our apartment is dingy by comparison.'

Loveday thought she noticed Abbie flick her companion an irritated look, then decided she might have imagined it. 'I was lucky to find this place,' she murmured.

Kit sank into the armchair, but Abbie remained standing.

'Would you like a drink? I've got tea, coffee . . . wine. What's it to be?'

Kit glanced hopefully at Abbie and she nodded. 'Tea would be fine,' she beamed.

In the kitchen, Loveday opened the new box of Earl Grey and took down the mugs. She'd also been looking forward to a hot shower, but it would have to wait.

'I see the police have identified the body in the cove,' Abbie called through. 'Did you know him?'

Loveday appeared with the tea and shook her head.

Bur Abbie wasn't ready to give up her subject. 'I wonder if they are any closer to finding the man who killed him?'

Loveday stiffened, remembering Lawrence, who as far as she knew, was still in police custody. 'Not as far as I know,' she said stiffly.

She saw the women exchange looks.

'Do you know something?' Abbie's voice was eager.

'No . . . I . . . They've been chasing a few false trails, that's all.'

'What kind of trails?' Kit asked, her eyes widening.

Loveday was on the point of telling them about Lawrence, but hesitated. She didn't know these women. They were strangers to her. If they were just being nosey, then it was ghoulish.

'I'm sorry,' Abbie interrupted her thoughts. 'You obviously don't want to talk about this . . . and we don't blame you. It was horrible.'

Out of the corner of her eye Loveday saw Kit shudder. Abbie was right. It had been horrible, but it was an ordeal that they had shared with her. She felt guilty for imagining their interest was unreasonable. 'The police have been questioning one of my friends,' she said quietly.

Abbie stiffened. 'They surely don't think he could have done this?'

'Of course not. They are just ruling him out of enquiries.'

Abbie was watching her closely. 'So they're letting your friend go then?'

'Not yet,' Loveday said. 'But they will.' She hoped she was right. She had no idea what another night in police cells would do to Lawrence.'

By the time the women left, Loveday's

appetite had returned and she cut herself a slice of ham and put two oatcakes on the plate, poured herself a glass of chilled Chardonnay and took the supper back through to the sitting room. Something was bothering her. She was trying to remember what it was, but she knew forcing the issue was hopeless. It would come to her when she was least expecting it. She had to find out why the police were still questioning Lawrence.

7

The Bentine's property was impressive. Loveday gave an appreciative whistle as Cassie's big green four-wheel-drive crunched up the drive and came to a halt by the front door. The place looked deserted.

'I think she's out,' Loveday said.

But Cassie frowned. 'No. She knows we're coming. I rang her this morning.'

As she turned off the engine the front door opened, and Magdalene came to meet them, leading them into a sitting room of antique elegance, where gilt framed pictures adorned the walls and two large cream sofas faced each other across a low glass-topped coffee table. Light flooded in from a high bay window that looked out over the front garden.

Magdalene Bentine was younger than Loveday had expected, or perhaps it was just her trim frame and fine boned face that gave the illusion of youth. When she spoke her voice was low and refined.

She indicated they should sit on one of the squashy leather sofas. 'Now, what would you like to drink . . . tea . . . coffee?' She glanced at the drinks' table behind the sofa. ' . . . Or something stronger?'

'Tea will be lovely,' said Cassie, speaking for both of them, ' . . . But later.' She patted the cushion beside her. 'Come and tell us how you are.'

Magdalene sat down and stared across the room, a far away look in her huge blue eyes. She shrugged. 'It's like a dream . . . I still can't take it in.'

Loveday studied her as she spoke. She couldn't imagine this fragile looking woman as the tough, successful business-woman Cassie had described. But people reacted differently to loss, and Magdalene had to deal with not only her husband's death, but knowing he'd been murdered.

'You shouldn't be here on your own,' Cassie was saying, her voice full of concern.

'Couldn't one of your family come to stay for a while?' Loveday interrupted.

'I have no family.' Magdalene bit her lip and her voice trembled. 'My father died before we left Cambridge. There's no one else.'

It was the first sign of sadness she had shown since Cassie and Loveday arrived. But it wasn't for her murdered husband. Magdalene Bentine was still grieving the loss of her father.

'Friends then?' Cassie cut in quickly.

'No, I'd rather be on my own.' She jumped as her mobile phone rang. It had been lying on the coffee table as though she had been expecting a call. She made a grab for it, but not before Loveday saw the name Martin flashing up. Magdalene clicked it off quickly and beamed an uneasy smile at them, 'Friends . . . ' she said with a shrug, 'they keep ringing . . . I'll get back to her.'

Loveday smiled. Magdalene's business was her own. But if she did have a man friend she didn't want others to know about then it might explain the lack of grief. She wondered just how happy the marriage had really been.

Magdalene was on her feet now. 'I don't know about you two, but I'm going to have a real drink.' She moved to the drinks' table and held the gin bottle aloft. 'Join me?' she invited.

Cassie and Loveday shook their heads and Magdalene poured a large measure of gin into a crystal glass and splashed tonic into it. Her mood had changed and Loveday wondered if it was the call from Martin that had raised her spirits.

Cassie was making moves to leave, but Loveday was reluctant to go before accomplishing the reason for her visit. She turned to Magdalene. 'Forgive me for asking at a time like this, but do you remember Lawrence Kemp . . . he's a friend of mine . . . an artist.'

Magdalene looked at her and frowned, trying to remember. Then her eyes lit up. 'Lawrence . . . Yes of course I remember him. What about him?'

'The police are holding him for questioning . . . maybe in connection with your husband's death.' The murder word was too stark to use.

Magdalene's eyes widened. 'Lawrence . . . kill Paul . . . never! They can't seriously believe that he had anything to do with this.'

'I know. It's ridiculous. I don't suppose he even knew your husband.' It was a shot in the dark, but she had to try.

'Oh, he knew him all right. It was Paul who defended him during his terrible court case.'

It was Loveday's turn to stare. Out of the corner of her eye she saw Cassie's mouth gape open. Magdalene put her hand to her mouth.

'I'm so sorry,' she said. 'I assumed you knew all about Lawrence's past . . . you being a friend of his, I mean.'

When they both shook their heads Magdalene raised her eyes to the ceiling trying to remember the details.

'It was a long time ago . . . when we all lived in Cambridge. There was an accident.' She shook her head sadly. 'A terrible accident. Lawrence had been driving and crashed his car. His passenger, a young woman was killed.' She sipped the glass of gin, hardly noticing it. 'It was worse . . . the woman had been expecting twins. None of them survived the crash.' She touched her temple as though that would help release details of the trial in her head.

'Paul represented him in court, but he pleaded guilty . . . death by dangerous driving . . . He was sentenced to eight years in prison.' She looked at the shocked expressions on Cassie and Loveday's faces. 'Poor Lawrence,' she said. 'I could hardly believe it, Cassie, when you recommended him to me to paint the Blue Lady.'

'You never said you already knew him,' Cassie gasped.

'No, it wasn't my business to bring up the past, anyway, he'd been punished enough. If Lawrence could make a new start here in Cornwall then I was certainly not going to spoil it for him. I didn't even tell Paul,' she added wistfully.

Loveday could feel herself warming to the woman. Lawrence would have appreciated Magdalene's discretion.

Loveday needed some thinking time to make some sense of everything. Could Sam Kitto really be putting Lawrence in the frame for a bizarre murder simply because he had known the dead man?

Back in her cottage that night Loveday

made a list of everyone she knew was connected to the case and then studied it. If there were any clues here then she couldn't see them. Her head hurt and her tummy rumbled. There was salmon in the freezer and went to prepare it for supper. While it was baking in foil she showered and put on her pyjamas. She deserved an early night.

Her mobile rang as she washed up after her meal, and she made a grab for it when she saw whose name was flashing. 'Lawrence! At last! Are you OK?'

'I'm fine, they've let me go.' His voice sounded flat and exhausted. 'I knew you'd be worried, but don't be because everything is fine now.'

'Where are you. Do you need a lift?' She looked down at her pyjamas.

'I'm still in Truro but the police are organising a car to take me home. I'm waiting for it now.'

She could hear him sigh.

'Can we meet up tomorrow? We need to talk.' He suggested the same pub where she'd had supper with Abbie and Kit.

'About noon?' Loveday suggested.

'Sounds great,' Lawrence said, and rang off before she had a chance to ask any more.

*   *   *

The pub car park was busy. Being close to the coastal cliff path it was a good stopping off place for walkers. She spotted Lawrence's battered old vehicle and pulled alongside it to park, before walking through the beer garden and around the building to the little door that led into the bar. He was sitting at a table in the furthest corner and got up, holding his arms out to Loveday as she walked in. He looked paler than usual and she guessed he hadn't slept much over the past few days.

'I'll get you a drink,' he said. 'What's it to be?'

'A glass of orange juice, please.'

She watched him at the bar as he waited for their drinks. He appeared older than when she had last seen him. Fragments of Magdalene's story flitted through her head. Loveday felt she was looking at a stranger.

'How much do you know?' he asked, putting her drink in front of her and sliding into the bench seat opposite

Loveday stared into the glass and imagined she could see her reflection in its contents. 'I know about the accident . . . and the prison bit.'

Lawrence sank back into his seat and stared at her, his eyes questioning. 'How . . . ?' he said, his brows drawing together. ' . . . How long have you known?'

'Since yesterday. Magdalene Bentine told us . . . Cassie and I, I mean. We went to see her.'

Lawrence was watching her face intently for any sign of anger . . . maybe even disgust, but he saw none. 'What exactly did she tell you?'

'That there had been an accident. That you were driving. That a woman in the car with you had been killed.'

He wondered if Magdalene had sweetened the pill by not mentioning the circumstances.

'Did she tell you about the babies? Did she tell you the dead woman had been expecting twins?'

Loveday nodded, her expression grim. A couple dressed in walking clothes brought their drinks to a nearby table and settled themselves down. Lawrence glanced uneasily at them.

'Let's walk, Loveday,' he said, reaching for his jacket.

They left the bar and took the rough track behind the pub that wound past ancient, boulder-strewn fields and ended by the cliff path. The air was bracing and tasted of salt. Loveday zipped her jacket against the wind, plucking at strands of dark hair that had blown across her face.

'This is quite a place,' he said, his eyes narrowing as he took in the expanse of wild terrain. The sea was to their right, waves crashing noisily over the rocks below. Suddenly Bentine's body was there again in her mind, a ghoulish image on that shingle beach. She looked away, trying to shut out the sea and the awful recurring horror it provoked.

Lawrence was still tracking the horizon, his eyes narrowed against the wind. 'Did you know it was Paul Bentine who represented me in court?'

She nodded.

'I was at Borlase the night he was killed.'

Loveday stared at him. Had she heard right. He couldn't have been at Borlase that night . . . he'd been with her at the gallery in St Ives . . . at his exhibition. That's what she had told the police. But Lawrence had arrived late . . . She remembered how moody and distant he had been all evening.

Her eyes never left his face. 'You didn't kill him, Lawrence! Tell me you didn't kill him!'

Lawrence let out a gasp. 'Of course I didn't kill him! I didn't even see him that night.'

'Then why?'

'It's a long story, but . . . in a nutshell, Bentine was blackmailing me.'

The path was close to the cliff edge and Lawrence picked up a stone and hurled it out into the surging sea.

'There was a letter,' he went on. 'Someone pushed it through my door. I thought it was from him.' He grimaced at the memory. 'It said if I didn't want my past to be made public then I had to meet the sender at the pub at Borlase that evening. I wanted to finish this thing with Bentine once and for all, so I went along. I sat there for half an hour nursing a pint, but no one turned up to meet me.' He shrugged. 'So I left.'

The wind whipped at Loveday's hair. 'I don't understand. What thing with Bentine?'

Lawrence zipped his jacket to his chin and turned up the collar, watching the waves cresting as they hit the rocks below.

'After prison, I came to Cornwall to start a new life. Nobody knew me here — and that's how I wanted it. I changed my name.' He looked at Loveday. 'I'm Lawrence Kennet.'

She swallowed as he described his meeting with Cassie on the beach at Marazion.

'Anyway, after that she put some more work my way . . . painting a picture of the Bentine's boat for one, although, at the time, I'd no idea it had anything to do with Paul Bentine. As far as I knew it was a commission from a local businesswoman, Magdalene Carruthers.

'The Blue Lady had a mooring down at Helford Passage at that time and I was doing the preliminary sketch from the beach when someone came up behind me. It was Bentine.

There was a large boulder on the path ahead and they sat on it.

'Bentine was threatening to blackmail me, Loveday.' He said flatly. 'He was quite blatant about it . . . said I could be useful to him. He was smiling . . . he said he could go to the police and tell them everything any time he wanted.'

Loveday's brows creased. 'I don't understand. How could he blackmail you about something the police already knew?'

But Lawrence smiled grimly and shook his head. 'The police didn't know everything.' He looked up at her, the strain etched on his face. 'You see, it wasn't me who crashed the car that day. I wasn't even there.'

Loveday's mouth dropped open, but she did not interrupt him.

'It was Anchriss,' he said softly, 'My wife.'

Lawrence had never mentioned a wife.

'She'd been drinking,' he continued.

'Normally she never touched the car when she was drinking, but this was an emergency. Meredith Teague — she and her husband, Brian had the cottage next door — came hammering on the door. She was in labour . . . the babies were coming and she was all alone. She was panicking and begging Anchriss to drive her to hospital.'

He spread his hands in a hopeless gesture. ' . . . And the rest is history. I was out in the woods sketching and heard the bang. Anchriss had been thrown clear and was hardly scratched . . . but Meredith. I told Anchriss to get off home and call an ambulance. Everyone just assumed that I was the driver, and I didn't tell them any different.'

He met Loveday's shocked eyes. 'I had to take the blame. Anchriss would have been crucified if she had gone to trial. You can imagine the headlines — Drunk driver kills expectant mother and her unborn twins!' He paused and gave an ironic laugh. 'It killed her anyway. My going to prison instead of her just increased her guilt. She hanged herself

. . . from the beam in our kitchen.'

He made no attempt to check the tears rolling down his face and Loveday had to blink hard to check her own smarting eyes. Her arms went round him and for a while they sat like that as the sea churned and tossed behind them. After a while they stood up and began walking slowly back to their cars.

'I had committed perjury, you see,' Lawrence said softly. 'And that's what Bentine was threatening to tell the police. I wasn't all that bothered about the prospect of going back to prison . . . but I couldn't allow him to blacken Anchriss's name.' He shook his head. 'I couldn't let him do that.'

'No, I can see that,' Loveday said quietly. 'And do the police now know all of this? Is that why they arrested you?'

'No, it wasn't actually. They found some kind of blackmail list at Bentine's place, and my name was on it. I don't think he could have added any details. I'm sure the police would have confronted me with them by now if they had known.

'But they did check me out. Took my

picture to the landlord of the Borlase pub and he identified me . . . told them it was me in his bar the night Bentine was murdered.'

'But surely that should have cleared your name. I mean, you could hardly have dragged Bentine down to that beach while you were sitting in the pub.'

Lawrence shook his head. 'I don't know if the police see it that way. I think they believe I killed him . . . but they just can't prove it.'

Loveday was horrified. ' . . . and they never will, because you're not guilty.' She took his arm as they neared the pub car park. 'Nobody but Bentine knew that Anchriss was driving that night?'

'Not as far as I know.'

'But somebody must have . . . and they have been trying to frame you.' She bit her lip. ' . . . There's more, Lawrence. Somebody vandalised your painting at the museum in Truro . . . sprayed it in red paint.'

'Christ,' he said. 'What's going on, Loveday?'

8

Loveday knew what she was going to do before she reached home that night. She would check out Cassie's story about the pub along the coast — and there was no time like the present. So, instead of turning down to Marazion, she carried on towards Land's End.

There were no signs of life, and cottage windows were firmly curtained as she drove through the tiny hamlet surrounding the pub. It too looked closed. She was kicking herself now that she hadn't rung ahead to make an appointment to interview the landlord. At least she had a name — Davie Richardson, the internet search had revealed.

No lights burned in the tiny windows facing the street, so she drove along the side into the car park. The sound of her car brought a small, ruddy-faced man out to investigate.

'We're closed,' he said, squinting out at her.

'I'm so sorry,' Loveday said, getting out and coming to meet him. 'Are you Mr Richardson?'

The light from the open back door showed the man to have a crop of crinkly grey hair. He narrowed his eyes. 'Do I know you?'

Loveday offered her apologies and explained who she was, saying she was interested in writing a feature about the pub's history.

The suspicious grey eyes sprung to life at the likelihood of free publicity. 'We've got half an hour before we open, so we'll have to be quick young lady,' he said, suddenly animated.

She followed him through the low back door, watching her step on the uneven flagged floor, into the public bar. He threw a light switch as he passed and the bar sprung into life. Fairy lights dangled from the optics. A wood-burning stove occupied a small inglenook fireplace and wall lights gave the room a cosy feel.

'I'll fetch some tea,' he said, indicating Loveday to a chair. There must have been a pot brewing for the landlord re-appeared almost immediately with two steaming mugs and a plate of biscuits.

'Well, fire away,' he said brightly, sliding a white china mug in front of Loveday.

'You don't mind this, do you?' Loveday held up the tiny voice recorder she used for interviews. 'It just helps to back up my notes.'

He shook his head, now looking like he was going to enjoy his new status as interviewee. 'Evie and I — that's my wife — have been here about . . . ' he looked up, mentally calculating the years, ' . . . about ten years now. It was our first pub. Not that it's always been easy, mind, but we do benefit from the tourist trade in the summer.' He nodded towards the ceiling. ' . . . And we have a couple of letting rooms.' He paused. 'One of them is haunted.'

This was more like it. Loveday raised an eyebrow. 'Now this is what I need to hear about,' she grinned encouragingly. 'Tell me more.'

Davie Richardson's chair creaked as he settled back into it. 'There's been an inn on this site for over 700 years,' he began.

'And I dare say bits have been added on over the centuries, but I believe it's basically the same. Locals say that in the old days it was the headquarters for smugglers and wreckers.' He sat forward and nodded to Loveday ' . . . and we have the old tunnels to back that up.'

She could imagine that, out here in this remote spot, with the wild Cornish seas thrashing all around, it was the perfect place for smugglers to hide their booty.

'In the old days, the villagers were told to turn their backs when the carts, carrying the brandy, silks and teas were trundled through the streets.' Davie Richardson continued, looking up to gauge whether Loveday was impressed by his tale. Satisfied that she was, he went on: ' . . . story goes, that a landlady of the time betrayed the smugglers to the authorities.' He sniffed. 'She was getting her own back you see, because the owner of the inn refused to let her and her husband stay on rent free.'

Loveday held her breath. 'The locals punished her,' Richardson continued, ' . . . by taking her down to the beach at low tide and pinning her there so that she drowned when the tide came in.' His eyes rose to the ceiling again. 'It's supposed to be her ghost up there,' he said.

A silence fell between them as the landlord allowed the drama of his story to take effect.

Loveday sat back, watching him. She could imagine him regaling the tourists with that tale. He'd probably told it to thousands before her. It might make a good seasonal article, but she'd hoped for more. Now she felt silly. It was ridiculous imagining she could discover some tangible link with Paul Bentine in this place. She stood up and Richardson's eyes followed her as she wandered around the bar, inspecting the pictures. She was drawn to a watercolour of the pub. 'This is nice,' she said, moving in for a closer look, then froze. The name scrawled in the corner was 'Kemp.'

'Nice chap that artist was,' Richardson said, ' . . . stayed with us for a bit.' He sniffed. 'Rent free, mind.'

Loveday turned and gave him a questioning look.

'Arrived on an old bicycle one day, backpack full of painting gear . . . offered to paint the pub in exchange for a few nights' board.' He nodded, remembering. 'Well, it was October and the rooms were empty, so Evie said why not. Stayed nearly a month, he did . . . helped out in the bar at night.' He nodded again. 'Yeah, nice chap he was.'

Davie Richardson had gone behind the bar to remove the towels from the beer pumps when the first customer walked in.

Loveday wheeled round and her eyes flew open. 'Detective Inspector Kitto! Well . . . fancy meeting you here.'

Sam grimaced. 'I might say the same.' He was looking at her as though he expected some kind of explanation, so she obliged.

'I've been interviewing the landlord . . . for a magazine feature.'

'Of course you have,' he said, looking away. Had she just seen the man smile?

'What can I get you, folks?' Davie Richardson was back in landlord mode. 'They're on the house.'

Sam raised his eyebrows at Loveday 'White wine?'

She nodded and he ordered the house white, adding a pint of dark beer for himself, which despite the protestations of the landlord, he insisted on paying for.

'OK,' he said, joining her at a table. 'Care to tell me why you're really here?'

She tilted her chin. 'I just did. I'm working.'

'So you're not interfering in my case then?'

The landlord had disappeared through to his own quarters, but Loveday still lowered her voice. 'You have to accept the Bentine murder looks like some kind of revenge attack. Whoever killed him went to an awful lot of trouble when a blade between the ribs could have done the job.'

Sam threw back his head and laughed. He looked different when he wasn't scowling. And she noticed again that his eyes were an attractive dark brown.

'And have you narrowed down the field of suspects for us?'

'If you're seriously asking for my opinion, inspector, I'd say this was a woman's crime. You know . . . hell hath no fury, and all that.'

'Have you any particular woman in mind?'

She had, but the idea was ridiculous. She'd actually liked Magdalene, but she was definitely hiding something. She sat up, lifting her glass. 'Isn't that your job? All I know for sure is that Lawrence had nothing to do with it.' She swallowed her wine. ' . . . And before you ask, he's told me all about his time in prison.'

Sam pursed his lips and tilted his head, his eyes never leaving Loveday's face. He knew he was intimidating her, but he indulged himself. She was opinionated and definitely interfering, but wasn't that what journalists did? Still, he shouldn't let his guard down.

He couldn't afford to be bewitched by those teasing hazel eyes, or even admit to this urge he had to run his fingers through that silky dark hair. He thought about her and Kemp and wondered again just what their relationship was. He'd watched the pair of them on the cliff top that morning and hadn't got the impression that they were a couple, but perhaps that was just wishful thinking on his part.

'How did you two meet?' He tried to keep his voice casual.

'It was an assignment Merrick gave me. I took pictures of some of Lawrence's paintings and wrote an article about him. When I mentioned I was looking for a place to stay he introduced me to Cassie and Adam.' She looked up, her hazel eyes serious. 'Lawrence Kemp is one of the kindest people I've ever met, inspector. He doesn't have a vindictive bone in his body. Just because he knew Paul Bentine doesn't mean he killed him.'

Sam tried to maintain a non-committal expression. The artist had been arrested because Bentine was blackmailing him — and because the landlord of the Borlase pub had identified him as having been there the night the lawyer was killed. They had no proof, of course, and Kemp had explained he'd had a letter instructing him to meet Bentine there that evening. The fact that the letter had never been found didn't exactly help his case. So no, Mr Kemp wasn't exactly off their radar — no matter how *kind* he was.

*   *   *

Loveday's head was buzzing as she drove back to the cottage. She knew Sam Kitto hadn't believed she'd been at the pub only to interview the landlord. But the fact that he'd also turned up must surely mean he was considering her theory. She hadn't put it into so many words, but it was a strong possibility that the killer had got the idea of murdering Bentine in that bizarre way after visiting the place and hearing its story. She'd been looking for proof that Magdalene knew the place, but had only succeeded in discovering it was Lawrence who'd stayed there.

The first thing she did when she got home was to get out her laptop. She typed Lawrence's real name into the search box and held her breath. The report of the court case flashed onto the screen and she read through it quickly. It was just as he'd described. She printed it and checked the next reference. There had been a bit of a backlash after the court case and Meredith's husband was threatening to get his revenge. There was a picture of an angry, grief-stricken young red-haired man. No one she recognised, but it was a start. He had threatened Lawrence after all.

Then came the newspaper report of Anchriss's sad death. The inquest, ignorant of the true events, had concluded that Anchriss took her own life in a state of deep depression with her husband in prison and her best friend dead. Poor Anchriss . . . poor Lawrence. But most of all, poor Brian Teague!

Loveday couldn't even imagine the despair he must feel at the loss of his wife, Meredith and their two unborn babies. Such a waste. She shook her head, feeling the wetness sting her eyes. Such a terrible tragedy . . . but shedding tears now would not help any of them. It certainly wouldn't find Paul Bentine's killer. She pushed the print button.

There was a lot more stuff about Bentine. It seemed he and Magdalene had a high profile in Cambridge society. She studied the picture of them at some posh dinner. He looked confident . . . arrogant . . . every inch the successful professional man. Successful he may have been, Loveday sighed, but only because he dabbled in other people's misery.

There were group pictures of the Bentines at other high-flying social events. This pair lived well. In another photo Magdalene was linking arms with an elderly man, whom Loveday assumed to be her father. He looked more the retired country gent than the revered Judge. She sat up stretching, and with a yawn closed the file. She would think clearer in the morning.

★　★　★

Magdalene was unable to control the feeling of rising panic. That image of Paul's bloated and lifeless body would haunt her forever. Bile rose in her throat and she clamped a hand over her mouth, concentrating on deep, reviving breaths until the retching stopped. She lay back on the bed, exhausted. She knew she had to play the grieving wife, but they would all see through her deception. Suddenly, she had an overwhelming need to hear Martin's voice. She focused on the little silver clock beside her bed. It was almost seven . . . too late to contact him. And what if his wife knew about their 'secret' mobile? If she rang him now maybe she would pick it up.

Magdalene went into her bathroom, turned on the shower, and seconds later was standing motionless beneath the cascade of piercing hot jets. They didn't refresh her. Still wet, she pulled on a bathrobe and wrapped a towel around her dripping hair. The eyes that stared back from the steamed up bathroom mirror weren't hers. This woman, with her grey pallor and sunken dark eyes, was a stranger.

Ten minutes later she was back on the edge of the bed. She'd been unable to resist calling him after all. 'But you must come round,' she pleaded, 'we need to talk about this!'

His voice had become muffled and she knew he had put his hand over the phone as he called through to his wife. 'It's one of the parishioners.' Then, more clearly, he said to Magdalene, 'Pull yourself together . . . look, we'll get through this . . . but not if you fall apart.'

9

Even before she opened the curtains Loveday could tell that it was a drizzly, grey morning. She peeked out and shivered at the bank of mist creeping across the bay. As she watched, the shape of the mount grew fuzzy until it was only a vague impression. It was the gloomy, dripping kind of morning that Loveday hated, but today it matched her mood. She'd gone to bed feeling emotionally drained and woken in a similar frame of mind. She plugged in the kettle before dragging herself to the bathroom for the daily showering ritual. Her head was thudding as she swallowed two Paracetamol tablets with a cup of Earl Grey tea and closed her eyes until her headache subsided. If Lawrence was to be cleared of any suspicion of this murder then she had to get a move on. Leaving it to Inspector Kitto didn't seem to be an option. She would prove his innocence — even if she had to solve the thing herself.

Cassie's back door opened when she heard Loveday leaving. She ran out in her dressing gown, rattling a small bunch of keys, and grimaced apologetically. 'You're not going into Truro by any chance?'

Loveday nodded.

'Could I beg a huge favour?'

Loveday heaved an exaggerated sigh and rolled her eyes skywards 'What now?' she joked.

'They're for the Blue Lady. I forgot to give them back to Magdalene.' She gave her an imploring look. 'I know it's an awful liberty . . . but I just wondered . . . if you happen to be in the area.'

Loveday grinned at her friend and reached for the keys. 'It'll cost you.'

'A glass of wine when you get back. How's that?'

'It'll do,' Loveday said, turning to wave as she put the car into gear and crunched down the drive.

The Bentine house was on the north side of the city and Loveday decided to call in on her way into the office. The misty drizzle had developed into a downpour by the time she joined the queuing cars waiting to negotiate the Chiverton roundabout. The Bentine file lay on the passenger seat beside her and as she glanced down at it, the terrible image down in the cove that day once again flashed into her mind. It was as though she was standing above it and could see the knots in the twine used to tie Bentine's wrists to the tent pegs that had been used to secure him to the beach. Someone had actually taken the man's body to the deserted cove — or maybe not. Maybe he'd been alive when he arrived there . . . gone willingly with his killer perhaps, ignorant of his imminent demise?

The traffic moved and Loveday edged the car closer to the roundabout. She forced herself to concentrate on the road ahead. But somewhere in amongst those newspaper cuttings by her side was the key that would unlock the whole mystery. The trouble was, she suspected that there might be more than one key. The trick would be to find the right one.

The traffic was moving again and she followed it onto the roundabout, taking the exit that took her down through the retail estates, past the hospital and the college, into the city centre.

She almost forgot about Cassie's errand and only remembered her promise to deliver the keys when she was nearing the city centre. She cursed, turning back at the next roundabout. Once off the main thoroughfare, the roads were quiet. It didn't take long to reach the secluded cul-de-sac where Magdalene lived.

But as she approached the corner she had to pull up to allow a police car to emerge. It was followed by another vehicle. Loveday studied them with interest then her eyes flew open. Magdalene Bentine was in the back of the second car. And she looked far from happy as she stared ahead, her back ramrod stiff.

Loveday's brow creased. Was Magdalene being arrested? She pulled into the side of the road, behind another parked car, while she thought about this. Maybe she was just going to help the police with their enquiries? But couldn't they have questioned her at home? She could be going in to look at photographs, to identify someone perhaps . . . so why the accompanying police car?

The clock on her dashboard was creeping past nine o'clock. She didn't want to be late again. Magdalene's involvement with the police was something she would have to think about later. She made a three point turn, realising as she did so that there was a man at the wheel of the parked vehicle. And if she wasn't mistaken, he was wearing a dog collar.

The traffic was heavy as Loveday drove into the centre. The electronically controlled gate into the magazine's private car park was open and she caught sight of Merrick's car just ahead. She followed him through the high iron gates, pulling into the space next to his. He was getting out and gave her a wave before pointing his key to lock his car. They exchanged greetings and walked together into the building and up to the editorial offices where Merrick paused before opening the door.

'Look Loveday,' he said. 'You can talk to me about it you know.'

'Talk about what?'

'Well you're obviously worried about something. Is it Lawrence? I thought he was in the clear now?'

For the first time since the murder Loveday realised the effect her behaviour must be having on the people around her. She'd been so worried about Lawrence, and now she seemed to have got herself involved with Magdalene Bentine. If she had thought about it she would have been more aware of the worried glances her colleagues were sharing. She'd been self-ish . . . maybe now was the time to unload some of her thoughts. Another point of view might help 'Actually, Merrick,' she said, 'there is something I would like to run past you.'

They went into his office giving nods in response to the curious glances as they passed through the main office. Merrick slipped off his coat and hung it carefully on the hanger at the back of his door. He went to his desk, indicating the chair opposite for Loveday. Then he sat, fingers steepled waiting for her to begin.

'Lawrence has done nothing wrong, you know.' She hadn't meant to sound so defensive.

Merrick shrugged. 'Did I say otherwise?'

'No, but you're looking as though you're

feeling sorry for me.' Her teeth caught at her bottom lip. 'He's a sweet, gentle guy, Merrick . . . and he doesn't deserve all this. It's just that there were things in his past that the police wanted to check.'

Merrick raised an eyebrow and Loveday wondered if Sam had discussed the case . . . discussed Lawrence . . . with him. They were friends, certainly, but surely a police officer was bound by some sort of confidentiality regarding the people they interviewed — especially when they were innocent? She could see Sam's face, his uncompromising dark eyes. He might be arrogant, certainly annoying, but she couldn't see him discussing a case with anyone other than a colleague.

'There are things I can't talk about; things Lawrence told me in confidence. But I am absolutely certain that he had nothing to do with Bentine's death.'

She studied Merrick's face for some indication that he believed her, but his expression was confused. How could she expect him to understand any of this when she wasn't sure herself what was going on?

Merrick was sitting back in his swivel

chair, hands now clasped behind his head, as he considered the situation. He frowned and pressed his lips together. 'If the police have released Lawrence then why are you still so worried, Loveday?'

'Because,' she said with a sigh, 'There is a connection.'

She saw Merrick's back straighten, but it was too late now to change her mind about telling him. 'I may as well tell you. Lawrence knew Bentine. When he lived in Cambridge, he knew him. Oh, what the hell, it's all out there on the internet anyway, if you know where to look. But for the moment I need your assurance not to repeat what I'm going to tell you.'

'Do you have to ask?'

'No, of course I don't. I'm sorry, Merrick. It's just me getting paranoid about this thing.'

Over the next ten minutes she recounted the details of the horrific accident and of how Lawrence had served five years in prison after admitting a charge of causing death by dangerous driving. She told him about the anonymous note that took Lawrence to Borlase Cove that evening . . . placing him at the murder location at the very time when Bentine was reported to have died. But Loveday didn't mention that Lawrence's confession at the time had been perjury. She was still trying to get her head round the fact that he had taken the blame for the tragic accident when, in fact, it had been his alcoholic wife, Anchriss, who had been driving that night.

Merrick listened, his expression thoughtful.

'So you see,' she said, shrugging. 'I have to help him. We have to prove he is completely innocent.'

Merrick's sigh was long and deep. 'You're on a crusade here, aren't you, Loveday?'

He leant across his desk to take her hand, and then remembered the rest of the editorial floor was probably keeping an interested eye on the pair of them.

'I suppose it's no use telling you not to get involved?'

Her look confirmed this.

'Don't antagonise the police, Loveday. Leave it to Sam and his crew. They know what they're doing.' He smiled wryly, 'Sam really is quite competent, you know.

If it's there, he will find it.'

'Actually,' she said innocently. 'There is more . . . I think they have arrested Bentine's wife . . . widow.'

Merrick's eyes widened and Loveday continued, 'I was up there this morning and saw them driving her off in a police car. She didn't look very happy about it.'

'I suppose it would be too much to expect you to tell me what you were doing there?'

Loveday told him about the keys to the Blue Lady as she fished them out of her bag.

'For goodness sake, Loveday,' he exploded. 'Why have you still got them? You have to hand these keys over right now! Take them to Sam . . . immediately!'

Loveday bit her lip and stared at the keys now lying on the desk between them.

'Don't even think about it!' he warned. 'Whatever is in your mind just forget it!'

'I just wanted a quick look at the boat again before handing them over.'

'You know, Loveday,' Merrick hissed, ' . . . sometimes I just don't believe you. Have you any idea what trouble you would be in if you went to that boat?' His eyes rolled to the ceiling. 'It could be a murder scene, for heaven's sake, and you are considering stumbling in . . . contaminating everything . . . '

Loveday stared at him. 'You think Bentine could have been killed on the boat?'

Merrick's hands spread in an expressive gesture that conveyed he had no idea. 'I don't know,' he said, his voice rising. 'But the point is . . . neither do you!'

Loveday was biting her lip again. 'You're right,' she said reluctantly. ' . . . But I have to let Cassie know first. She's the one who had the keys, after all.'

'Do it now,' Merrick ordered. ' . . . Then take the keys to Sam . . . and don't give him any hint that you even considered doing otherwise.'

Truro's Piazza was buzzing. Since its rebirth as a community space from the city's former bus station, the vast area was used for all kind of public entertainment, from carnivals to charity events. The annual food festival was to take place that coming weekend and a big green and white marquee had been erected overnight in readiness. The area was littered with

165

contractors' vehicles and men in dark blue overalls were hammering together staging, erecting scaffolding poles and unloading tables into the marquee. Resisting the urge to join the growing audience watching the activities, Loveday skirted round them and cut down into Green Street on her way to the police station. If DI Sam Kitto were any kind of copper he would be grateful to her for handing over these keys. So why did she have this nagging feeling that her turning up out of the blue would only antagonise him again?

The young constable at the reception desk eyed her with disinterest as she walked in 'DI Kitto, please.' She told him curtly.

'Can I say what it's about?' he said, trying to sound like he cared.

'Just tell him Loveday Ross is here . . . about the murder.'

The constable's head snapped up and he stared at her. 'Murder?' he said. 'What murder would that be?'

'Oh, for heaven's sake,' Loveday snapped. 'Is he in or not?'

The officer picked up a phone punched at a keypad and, after a few seconds, said.

'A Miss Ross to see you, sir. Something about the murder investigation.'

He looked up at Loveday and nodded as though the person at the other end of the line could see him. 'Very good, sir.'

He opened a drawer under the counter and produced a red visitor's badge. 'Pin this on,' he instructed. ' . . . And somebody will be down to collect you.'

After five or six minutes a woman a few years older than herself strode into the reception area. She arched an eyebrow in Loveday's direction. 'Miss Ross?'

Loveday nodded and stood up.

'I'll take you up to the CID room,' she said.

They walked side by side along a corridor and up a flight of stairs and through another set of doors before stopping and entering what looked like any busy office. If she had been a different kind of journalist, working on a newspaper, she would probably have been familiar with the inside of the local police station. But neither she nor her colleagues at the magazine had any call to visit here. The office she was being led through was noisy and buzzing.

Some people had phones clamped to their ears, others tapped busily into computers and the rest seemed to be reading or thumbing through papers on their desks. Loveday recognised a few of the faces that turned in her direction as she followed the woman through the CID section, and some of them nodded to her.

The door to DI Kitto's office was open and she could hear his voice as he sat at his desk talking to someone on the phone. He looked up as they entered and signed for Loveday to take the vacant chair opposite. Loveday imagined she had seen the trace of a smile as he ended his conversation and put the phone down, but his look was curious. Loveday fished the keys out of her bag and put them on the desk between them. Sam raised an eyebrow.

'They're the keys to the Bentine's boat . . . I thought you should have them.'

Sam sat up, staring at the two small keys on the key ring, but made no move to touch them.

'Just how did you come by these?' He met Loveday's eyes and his expression was hostile.

'Don't shoot the messenger. I'm just delivering them.' She shuffled uneasily in her chair. The keys were obviously important. 'Cassie, my landlady,' she explained, 'worked for Magdalene Bentine, — or Carruthers, as she calls herself professionally — anyway she runs this design business refurbishing the interiors of yachts. Magdalene was a client. Cassie had the keys last weekend to put the finishing touches to the refurb but forgot to hand them back when we went to see her that day.'

Sam's look was incredulous. 'You're telling me that your landlady has had these keys all this time and never thought they might be important?' His voice was rising and he was making an effort to control his anger.

Loveday looked up. Was it possible that DI Kitto had not known about the Blue Lady? Surely not. His team was questioning everybody concerned with the couple. She stared at the angry brown eyes.

'You did know about the Blue Lady, didn't you?'

The muscles along Sam's jaw were

working. He was trying to control his fury. 'You still haven't explained how you come to be in possession of these keys.'

Loveday shrugged. 'I was delivering them for Cassie, but when I got to the Bentines' house this morning Magdalene was being driven away by some of your lot.'

His eyebrows rose a fraction and Loveday jumped to the defence of her friend. 'Cassie's very good at what she does. She showed me a picture of the Blue Lady's interior before the makeover. The difference she made was amazing . . . '

Sam shook his head in disbelief. 'You've been *on* this boat?'

'Cassie took me down to Falmouth Marina to see how the other half live.'

He was watching her, his brows knitted, and Loveday continued uncomfortably, 'She had a few things to check out on board before handing the boat back to her client, she just wanted some company . . . what was the harm?'

'Are you forgetting that the owner of that boat has been murdered?'

The significance was not lost on Loveday. 'But we didn't know then about the connection with Bentine,' she reasoned. 'At that point he had not been identified as the murder victim, and in any case, Cassie only knew her client as Magdalene Carruthers.'

'So,' Sam said, his eyes still glinting with anger, 'The pair of you were stumbling about on the boat, touching things, moving things about?' he released a long exasperated sigh and reached for his phone.

'Jenny? Can you come through?'

He replaced the receiver but the phone immediately rang again. It was the front desk. He looked at Loveday as he asked the caller to hold. 'You'll have to be fingerprinted — you and your friend . . . if you don't have any objections, that is?'

His tone left little option for objection. Loveday knew it was necessary to eliminate her and Cassie from the police investigation. She nodded as the officer he called Jenny appeared and was instructed to organise the taking of her fingerprints.

Sam watched his detective lead Loveday out of his office. 'Send him up,' he instructed into the phone, but a tiny pang of guilt had crept in as he watched the women leave. It wasn't the young journalist's fault if his team was so blundering they couldn't even discover basic fact . . . like the affluent Bentines owning a yacht! They should have known about the boat . . . *He* should have known about it. Heads would roll for this one — and he had a feeling it would be his. The keys still lay where Loveday had placed them on his desk. He got up and went to the door and beckoned to Will to come through.

'Boss?' Will said, following Sam back into his office.

Sam pointed to the keys. 'The keys are for Bentine's boat. He has a bloody boat, Will . . . and none of us knew about it!'

Will hissed an expletive and put up his hands defensively. 'Sorry boss. How did we miss that?'

'That's what I'll be asking . . . I promise you,' he warned, ' . . . not to mention them.' He jerked a thumb upwards in the direction of the top brass who resided on the top floor of the building. He took a deep breath to control his temper. 'Get these checked for prints — and every other bloody check you can think of. Then I want you and the rest of the team down at the Falmouth marina.

'What about Magdalene Bentine?' he asked. 'What do you want us to do about her, boss?'

Sam had been on the point of going through to interview Magdalene himself when Loveday turned up. 'Well for a start I'll be asking why she didn't tell us about that damned boat. Has she said anything else yet?'

Will shrugged, 'Not a thing. She's got her solicitor with her now . . . refused to be interviewed until he got here.'

Sam frowned. 'The front office is sending someone up to see us. Says he has information about the case. He's a vicar.'

Will's eyebrows rose.

'I think we should see him before I interview Mrs Bentine,' Sam said.

10

The man in the dog collar gave Loveday a cursory nod as he passed her in the corridor. Her eyes fell to the visitor's card pinned to his jacket lapel. *The Rev Martin Foyle*. She frowned, trying to work out why the name should seem familiar. There would be plenty of men called Martin in Cornwall, but she'd seen the name recently. Then it came to her . . . Magdalene's mobile phone that day in her house. The name she had moved so quickly to cancel before Loveday or Cassie saw it was Martin. But she'd no reason to believe it was this man. On the other hand, it had been a vicar she'd noticed sitting outside Magdalene's house that morning. It had to be more than a coincidence.

'Mr Foyle?' Sam smiled as he stood to greet his visitor, extending his hand to indicate he should take the chair so recently vacated by Loveday. 'You have some information for us?'

Martin cleared his throat and glanced uneasily at Will, who had taken a place by the window. The tiny office seemed crowded and Martin felt a rising sense of claustrophobia. He ran a finger around the inside of his dog collar and gave Sam an appealing look. 'Can we speak . . . ' he glanced again at Will. ' . . . In private?'

Sam nodded for Will to leave the room and he went out, closing the door behind him. Sam settled into his chair. But for the dog collar he would never have taken Martin Foyle for a clergyman. He was too big for a start. Vicars in his day were older, smaller. He chided himself for the ridiculous notion. But the man was too tanned, too good looking . . . and a lot younger than Sam. Things were different now and dusty old academics in the pulpit were a thing of the past. Young clergymen attracted young congregations. As he watched him, the Rev Martin Foyle steeled himself to explain the purpose of his visit.

Sam raised an eyebrow. 'How can we help you, sir?'

Martin cleared his throat again and pressed tanned fingers to his temples. 'It's about Mrs Bentine,' he said.

Sam inclined his head, inviting the man to continue.

'We're friends, you see.' He spoke hesitantly.

'Friends?'

Martin's mouth was dry. He felt uncomfortable under the policeman's scrutiny. 'She's here, isn't she . . . here at the police station? You think she had something to do with her husband's death . . . Well, she didn't . . . she couldn't have.' Now that he'd started he seemed unable to halt the torrent of words that poured out. 'I should have come in days ago to tell you this. I let her down . . . let everybody down . . . my family.' His eyes looked wet and he swiped angrily at them.

Sam said nothing. He knew that to interrupt the man now might result in his clamping up.

'She couldn't have had anything to do with Paul's death because . . . she was not even in Cornwall at the time.' He looked up and waved a hand at Sam. 'Oh, I know she told you she was staying with friends in Bodmin, and they probably backed her up . . . but that was rubbish.' He paused, as though trying to select the right words, then looked up defiantly. 'She lied to you . . . because she was trying to protect me. You see, we were together all last weekend at the Bell Hotel in Frome. We hardly left our room.' He shot Sam a guilty glance. 'I think the staff will remember us.'

He sat back heavily, as though the revelations had exhausted him. But there was a spark of triumph in his eyes as if telling his story had somehow purged his soul. He'd come clean about his affair with Magdalene and was feeling better about it.

'Lying to the police is never a good idea,' Sam said sternly, as he scribbled the Bell Hotel, Frome, on his notepad. 'Especially when those officers are conducting an enquiry into a particularly callous and vicious murder.'

Martin flushed. 'Don't blame Magdalene . . . blame me. She lied to protect me . . . I'm . . . I'm married.'

'I don't imagine your congregation would be particularly delighted either to know about your extracurricular activities.' Sam's brows came down. He'd said too much. It was none of his business what this man got up to in his private life, so long as it didn't hamper his investigation.

Martin shook his head. 'Will you tell them?' But he didn't wait for an answer. 'I don't suppose it matters much now if you do. My career's finished . . . maybe even my marriage. I've let everybody down.' He met Sam's eyes, 'I'm not proud of myself.'

Martin's shoulders slumped. He looked like a broken man. Sam felt sorry for him. 'If this has no bearing on the case,' he said stiffly, 'then what you have told me needn't go any further. Of course, it's up to you what you tell your family.' He stood and extended his hand, indicating the interview was over.

Martin held his hand in a firm grip. 'I don't suppose I could see Magdalene?'

Sam shook his head.

'But you will let her go now?' Martin pleaded. 'She's done nothing wrong.'

'If the alibi you have just given her checks out then yes, she will be free to go. She was only ever here to answer a few questions.'

As the man moved to the door, Sam had a sudden thought. 'Did you know Paul Bentine, by the way?'

Martin stared at the floor. How could he forget? 'I met him once. It wasn't pleasant,' he said. 'I had called at Trenmere one evening when Mags and I both thought Bentine was to be away on business. But he answered the door himself. Magdalene's the quick thinking one. She rushed in and said she had asked me call to collect some jumble. Then she disappeared upstairs to throw a few things in a bag. Paul and I were left smiling at each other by the front door. He invited me in and we stood sipping sherry and making small talk. He was asking about the jumble sale, when it was and where, that kind of thing . . . and grinning'. He frowned, and looked up at Sam. 'It was an uncomfortable experience. Then Magdalene came back with some things for me to take away and I finished my sherry and took my leave of them.' He grimaced. 'I can still remember how much I was shaking when I got back outside the house.'

'Do you think he suspected there was something going on between his wife and you?'

'I don't know. It was all a bit surreal. I kept waiting for him to accuse us, but he didn't . . . then I thought he couldn't know. He wasn't the kind of man you would want to get on the wrong side of.'

'What do you mean?'

'He was vindictive. He treated Magdalene very badly.'

'You mean he was violent towards her?' Magdalene had given his officers no reason to believe she was an abused wife.

'No, his abuse was more subtle, more psychological. He knew how to twist things to cause the most distress. He was a thoroughly horrible man, Inspector . . . and I'm not surprised that someone murdered him.'

When Foyle had left, Sam called Will back into his office and repeated the vicar's story.

'I'll get it checked out right away, boss,' he said. 'What about Mrs Bentine? Do we let her go?'

Sam had his back to him and was standing at the window watching the traffic filing onto the roundabout below. 'Let's see if she fancies a trip to Falmouth,' he said.

The police forensic team had been sent ahead to do their work before Sam and the others went on board. Magdalene sat stiffly in the back of the Mazda that Will had collected from the available vehicles in the station car pool. They hadn't told her of Martin's visit but they no longer seemed to be treating her as a suspect. She stared disinterestedly at the fields rushing past. They'd told her she was free to go, but asked if she would take them to the boat. They'd seemed annoyed she hadn't mentioned the Blue Lady's existence. But Magdalene couldn't see why that was important. What could that possibly have to do with Paul's murder? It had happened miles away from the marina in Falmouth. The big good-looking one had been persuasive when he suggested that she should accompany him and the others to the marina. Magdalene just wanted the whole horrifying nightmare to be over. If taking them to the marina and showing them the Blue Lady would help, then she was happy to do it.

They avoided the congested Church Street and Arwenack Street, where most of Falmouth's shops were situated. The pubs strung out along their long lengths were favoured by the tourists because of their breathtaking views across the harbour to Flushing and the Carrick Roads. Instead, Will took the back road over the top of Falmouth, cutting down to the harbour and marina at the far end.

Magdalene could now make out the towering mass of two tankers tied up by the quays. A great white cruise ship was alongside another quay, while closer to shore, the masts of yachts bobbed in the marina. She directed them to the parking area and led the way along the pontoon. Out of the corner of her eye she could see the detectives looking around them at the boats in the marina, taking in the surrounding display of wealth. She stopped at an end berth and extended a hand towards the vessel bobbing at its mooring rope.

'This is my boat, The Blue Lady,' she said, but I suppose you already know that.'

Sam could see movement at the windows and knew that some of the team was still on board.

It was all Will could do not to release a long, slow whistle. The yacht was beautiful. A sleek hundred grand at least, he estimated. On his wages he probably couldn't even manage a rowing boat.

A figure in white overalls emerged to greet them. 'We're just about finished, sir. It's fine to go on board, now.'

They stood back, allowing Magdalene to step onto the moving deck, which she did with the confidence of a professional sailor. Sam and Will followed, steadying themselves on the handrail. She had reached the open door and was now waiting for them to descend into the cabin.

The smell of polished mahogany reached them before they had even climbed down. The Blue Lady's interior was as luxurious as Sam had imagined. He was not a boat person. His experiences of being afloat were limited to one outing on a tiny motorboat, and that had been for his son, Jack's, benefit. There had been another rather queasy trip on an angling boat during a holiday spent in Scarborough. The fishing had been good that day, Sam remembered — at least for everybody else on board. He'd spent most of his time hanging over the side. But what did they expect from a course fisherman. Not even the sumptuous surroundings of the Bentine's yacht could tempt him back to sea . . . not for a pleasure trip anyway.

The two forensic officers on board were packing up their equipment and nodded as the others squeezed past them.

'We'll be off now, sir,' one of them said, raising an arm as he climbed the steps to the deck.

'Thanks chaps,' Will called after them.

Sam had already started to look around. 'Did your husband keep any of his business papers here, Mrs Bentine?'

'No. Why would he? Paul kept all of that stuff under lock and key at home.' She threw Sam a look that said, 'You should know, you've been through them all.'

Sam ignored the intended scold as he caught sight of the desk and made his way to it. 'Mind if we have a look?'

Magdalene shrugged. 'Why not? I have nothing to hide. Look where you want to.' She reached into a cupboard above a tiny gleaming stainless steel hob and produced a jar of coffee. 'Want some?' she asked.

Both men nodded their approval and Magdalene produced a kettle from another cupboard, filled it over a dinky little sink and set it to boil on a gas flame.

Will was busy going through cupboards, opening drawers and checking out the space beneath the seating arrangements that he knew could convert into beds. He was fascinated by the ingenuity of the designers who hadn't wasted one inch of cabin space.

'I could probably help if I knew what you were looking for,' Magdalene said as they drank their coffee.

'We're looking to solve your husband's murder.' Sam's words were blunt. If they actually knew what they were looking for they might stand a better chance of finding it . . . of finding anything that would help them.

Will shot him a look of surprise and Sam immediately regretted his sharpness with the woman. He smiled in an attempt to lighten the atmosphere. 'We're almost finished here.' He hesitated then went on, 'Is it possible that your husband could have hidden something on the boat?'

'Like what?'

Sam shrugged. 'I don't know . . . a file perhaps . . . maybe a diary? We didn't find one at the house.'

Magdalene's brow creased as she tried to think. 'I've never known Paul to use a diary . . . well not since we moved to Cornwall. He put all his appointments on his computer, but I suppose he could have had a diary. I don't see why he would want to keep it here.' She pursed her lips and glanced around the cabin. 'You're right, though. He could be quite secretive . . . liked to make a mystery of things, a bit paranoid about anyone reading his papers. He wasn't keen on me finding out about any of his little projects, but he always had some deal or other going on.'

'I thought he was retired?' Will's head emerged from his inspection of the loo.

'He didn't practise law any more, if that's what you mean . . . not since we left Cambridge.'

'Why did you leave?' Sam asked.

'Good question,' Magdalene said. 'It just didn't suit Paul to live there anymore. But I've already told you all this.'

'Didn't you have a say in it?'

'Well, my father had died and I wasn't particularly happy. It didn't seem to matter much where we lived. It's true, all my friends were in Cambridge and my business was just beginning to take off. But Paul persuaded me that I didn't need to lose touch with them. 'Think of all those wealthy new clients you'll find down there,' he said. Anyway, he per-suaded me to move with him.' Her eyes had a faraway look. 'Paul was good at that. He had persuasion down to a fine art.' She looked around the cabin and smiled, 'I didn't need persuading about the sailing down here, it's great in Cornwall.' She stretched her arms wide. 'And I love my boat.'

An hour later, with coffee mugs washed and stored on their hooks back in the cupboard, Sam was beginning to doubt there had ever been anything to find. Then he had an idea.

11

Cassie had insisted on Loveday joining the family for supper. 'Nothing fancy, mind,' she said, 'just macaroni cheese, but it's the children's favourite.'

'Mine too,' Loveday confessed, as she allowed herself to be drawn into the warm kitchen. 'But I've really only come to tell you about the keys. I don't want to intrude.'

'Rubbish,' said Cassie, with a grin that told her it wasn't negotiable. 'You're one of the family now, so get busy in that cutlery drawer and set the table.'

She could hear the children in the next room and smiled. Judging from the high-pitched squeals and excited laughter, some kind of rough and tumble was going on. From time to time, Adam's voice rose above the others and it was difficult to tell who seemed to be enjoying the rumpus most.

'I know,' Cassie said, catching Loveday's amused expression. 'He's probably giving them piggybacks. What would his patients think if they could see him now?'

'That he's a great family man?'

'Great big kid, more like,' Cassie grinned, ' . . . but we all love him.'

Delicious aromas were filling the kitchen and Loveday put the finishing touches to setting the oversized wooden table where the family ate all their meals.

'What's the latest on the delectable Inspector Sam, by the way? Have you discovered any more about his marital status?'

'He's divorced. Merrick told me.'

Cassie raised an eyebrow. 'Children?'

Loveday nodded. 'A boy and a girl. They live with their mother in Plymouth.'

'And does he still see the kids?'

'Heavens, Cassie, I don't know. That's his business, don't you think.'

Cassie was lifting the bubbling dish from the oven and placing it carefully in the centre of the table. 'Don't get testy. I'm only asking.'

Loveday sighed. 'I know, but if you'd seen how furious he was that we were both on the Bentines' boat and hadn't bothered to tell them about it . . . ' A memory of Sam's angry brown eyes flitted into her head. Why did she always manage to antagonise him? 'Oh, and by the way, the police will need your fingerprints.'

'Really?' Cassie said. 'How exciting.'

She lifted the big silver serving spoon and started to dish up the food as she called for the others to come through. Squeals and laughter preceded their arrival and Loveday hugged the children in turn as she shepherded them to the sink to wash their hands.

'Do I get one too?' Adam teased, his round face flushed from the boisterous games.

'Don't see why not,' laughed Loveday, going forward with her arms outstretched.

'OK. One hug's enough,' said Cassie, brandishing her spoon.

'I suppose you'll be wanting one too,' Adam said teasingly, and pecked his wife's cheek.

Loveday thought they were the happiest family she had ever known.

Clearing away the supper things was a joint affair, with Adam washing, Loveday wiping and Cassie putting away. When the chore was done, Adam ushered the children upstairs and the sounds of more noisy squeals and splashing drifted through the open door of the sitting room where the women had settled themselves in front of the fire with replenished wine glasses.

'This is the life,' said Cassie, stretching luxuriously in the warmth of the room. 'It's the time I look forward to most . . . our respite after all the day's work.' She looked at Loveday. 'What about those keys then?'

'Yes . . . that's what I came to tell you.' Loveday settled herself back into the comfy armchair. 'I was going to return them on my way into the office, but there was a bit of a hitch. When I got to Magdalene's road, two police cars were just driving off.' She paused for effect. 'And *she* was in the back of one of them.'

Cassie put down her glass and stared at Loveday. 'You mean they've arrested her?'

'Looked very much like it to me.' Loveday waved her glass in the air. 'Well, you can imagine, I didn't know what to do. Honestly Cassie, I was shocked. But she has been behaving a bit suspiciously, don't you think? Well, for a start, she doesn't exactly look grief-stricken.'

Cassie shook her head. 'I think you're imagining things, Loveday. Magdalene couldn't have anything to do with all this, but go on.'

Loveday took a breath. 'I pulled in just before the entrance to her drive and sat there for a minute or two. That's when I noticed this other car. It was parked at the end of the cul-de-sac, and it drove off when I left. I could be wrong, but it looked like the driver had been waiting for the police to go.'

'Nosey neighbour, probably,' Cassie said.

'Maybe. But the driver was a vicar.'

Cassie's eyes were mocking. ' . . . And that was interesting because?'

'Well because I just happened to see him again an hour or so later — at the police station.'

'Vicars turn up at times of trouble. That's their job,' Cassie pointed out. 'Magdalene probably called him for support, or something, and he was following them to the police station.'

'So why did it take him an hour to get

there? And that's not all. He passed me in a corridor at the station and that plastic identity thing they make all visitors wear was pinned to his lapel.'

'And you just happened to squint at it as he passed?'

Loveday gave her an impish grin. 'I'm not a trained journalist for nothing. Anyway, his name is the Rev Martin Foyle. Do you know him?'

'Know who?' Adam asked as he walked into the room having read the compulsory bedtime story.

'The Rev Martin Foyle. Do you know him, Adam?' Loveday repeated.

Adam's brow creased as he considered this. 'Sounds familiar,' he said. 'If he's the one I'm thinking of . . . youngish chap, quite good-looking . . . he's got a parish in Truro. Saint something or other.'

'St Barnabas. I checked.'

Cassie's eyebrow rose and Loveday ignored it. 'The thing is, I think he called Magdalene the day we were there, Cassie, and she couldn't cancel the call fast enough. But I saw the name that came up on her phone, it was Martin.'

'Even if it was the same man, what would be wrong with a vicar calling his parishioner?'

'Well, nothing, but why would she want to hide the fact?'

Cassie met her eyes and a slow smile spread across her face. 'You're thinking they were having an affair,' she said, pointing an accusing finger at Loveday.

'Well it could be, couldn't it?' Loveday reasoned. ' . . . And if they were having a . . . thing . . . then Paul could have found out about it and been blackmailing the Rev.' Cassie and Adam stared at her in astonishment and she went on, 'Well it's not the kind of thing a vicar should be getting up to, is it? You can understand why he would want to keep something like that quiet. But the point is,' Loveday was getting into her stride now. 'It might give Magdalene a reason for wanting to do away with her husband.'

'Whoa there.' Adam put down the glass he had just filled. 'That's a pretty big assumption.'

'Adam's right, Loveday. You can't go round accusing people like that.'

'But you do agree that it's a possibility?' Loveday registered the look that passed between them and knew they were considering her logic.

'The thing is, I've discovered a bit more about Paul Bentine.' She had a captive audience now and continued. 'Put it this way. I'm positive that Lawrence didn't murder him, so I've been doing a bit of research. I believe Bentine had been blackmailing people. You see, it's not so far fetched to think he may have been blackmailing this vicar.'

Cassie, who'd been sitting with her legs tucked under her, wriggled into a more comfortable position in the chair. 'Have you told your friendly policeman any of this?'

'If you mean DI Kitto, well, no . . . I've.'

Loveday was interrupted by the trill of her mobile phone and she reached into her bag for it. She didn't recognise the number, but the voice was familiar enough. 'Inspector Kitto.' She made a face at the others. 'What can I do for you?' There was a pause while she listened. 'Cassie? Yes, I'm with her now.' She handed the phone across, opening her palms in a gesture of ignorance. 'He wants to speak to you, Cassie.'

Adam rose to sit on the arm of his wife's chair and Loveday tried to look as though she was not listening intently as Cassie took the call.

'Ah, Mrs Trevillick.' Sam's voice was urgent. 'I know this might seem a bit irregular, but we could do with your help.'

Cassie nodded, her expression puzzled as she wondered what was coming next. With Loveday's theories about Magdalene and the Rev Martin Foyle very much in mind Cassie bristled. If the police imagined she was going to pass on tittle-tattle about Magdalene then they had the wrong woman. But the detective's next words squashed those concerns.

'We're here with Mrs Bentine . . . on her boat.'

Astonishment crept into Cassie's voice. 'The Blue Lady . . . but what are you doing there?'

'It's alright, Cassie.' Magdalene had come to the phone. 'The police have this idea that Paul may have hidden something on board . . . something that could help them find his killer.'

'I don't understand. How does that concern me?'

'Just a minute. Here's the inspector. He'll explain.' She handed the phone back to Sam as Cassie, Adam and Loveday exchanged bewildered looks.

He wasted no time in pleasantries. 'When you were working on the boat, Mrs Trevillick, did you come across anything that struck you as unusual?'

'You mean some sort of hiding place? The work I did on the Blue Lady was purely cosmetic, Inspector, nothing structural.'

'Nevertheless, I would be grateful if you could just think back. Did you, for instance suspect there might be any false panels?'

'You mean secret compartments, false drawers, that kind of thing? Isn't that all a bit far fetched?'

She was right. Sam knew he was clutching at straws, but the man had been devious, and Sam had this feeling . . .

'Wait a minute,' Cassie said, 'There was something about measurements being out of line, if I remember right. It was to do with the bunks in the forward salon. The sides should have been identical, and we had the fabric cut to that specification. But when it was fitted, one side was out by about four inches. I remember I was annoyed because I was sure they had made a mistake in the cutting, but it wasn't that at all and we had to reorder the covers.'

'Which side?' Sam asked curtly.

'It was the right side that was out of line.'

'Thank you Mrs Trevillick, you've been very helpful.' Sam's voice was steady but he could feel the stab of excitement rising inside him.

With Magdalene's permission the two detectives made a detailed examination of the area Cassie had mentioned. They removed the cushions and began to inspect the interior. The floor was screwed down.

'I don't suppose . . . ' Sam started hopefully, but Magdalene had anticipated his request.

'You'll be needing a screwdriver. I'll fetch the toolkit,' she said, and disappeared back up the stairs to the deck of the boat. She returned a few minutes later carrying a red canvas pouch.

Sam hoped the others were not noticing the slight shake of his hands as he unscrewed the floor panel. All three held their breath as he lifted it clear to reveal a black metal security box.

Magdalene gave a sharp intake of breath and steadied herself. 'What is it?' she asked in a whisper.

'Something your husband obviously didn't want anyone to know about.' He pulled on a pair of plastic forensic gloves, and then selected two spanners from the toolkit to manoeuvre the box out of its resting place and onto the cabin floor.

'I suppose it's locked,' Magdalene said, her voice suddenly shaky.

Sam nodded. He could see a tiny keyhole. But he suspected it might take more than just a key to release the secrets of this box. However, finding the key would be a start.

He turned to Magdalene, reluctant to tell her what he must. 'I'm afraid we will have to impound your boat now, Mrs Bentine.'

But her look was resigned. She nodded.

'I understand,' she said softly.

Not for the first time in this inquiry Sam found himself admiring this woman's pluck. She'd lost her husband, even if he was a monster, and found herself in the middle of a murder inquiry — potential suspect even. Her affair with Martin Foyle was surely at an end, and now they were to deprive her of her one remaining pleasure — the Blue Lady.

'We'll release the boat as soon as we can. I promise,' he said.

Magdalene shrugged and gave him a weak smile. 'I know you will, Inspector.'

He turned to Will, who was already fishing in his jacket pocket for his mobile. 'It's alright boss, I'm on to it,' he said, punching keys.

'The whole crew, Will,' Sam instructed. 'We need everybody back down here. You know what to do. I'll take Mrs Bentine home.'

He took the main road through Falmouth this time. The shops were closed now and the streets quiet. The few tourists still about at this time of year had made their way back to their hotels or gone in search of restaurants and cafes for their evening meals. The thought reminded Sam that he had not eaten since breakfast. But food would have to come later. As they neared Truro he was remembering a second tiny computer memory stick they'd found in Paul Bentine's desk drawer. It had been checked, but there were no files or any trace of information ever having been stored on it. Believing it to be a spare, they had simply bagged it and put it in the evidence box. But Sam was now picturing the tiny silver key attached to it, thought at the time to have been of no importance.

He pulled into Magdalene's drive and drew up at the front steps. The hall light was on and he nodded towards it. 'Were you expecting company?'

Magdalene gave him a stiff-lipped smile. 'Security light. There's no one home.'

He felt guilty about leaving her alone here and offered to send for a family liaison officer, but she shook her head. 'No. I'll be fine. Anyway, I need some time on my own. I've a lot of thinking to do.'

He nodded to her as she got out of the

car. 'I'll be in touch,' he called from the open driver's window as he drove off.

When he reached the station, Sam headed straight for the Evidence Room. He wanted another look at that computer stick. He was itching to try the key in the lock of Bentine's box, but something stopped him. Through the evidence bag, his fingers felt a blister in the black lacquered finish. Curious, he turned the box over. It was odd that such an expensive security box would have a blemish. He pressed the blister and a section of the underside slid back, revealing a number pad. So . . . the key alone would not open this little box of tricks. He pressed the blister again and the panel slide closed, leaving no hint of its existence.

This was definitely one for Arthur Charlton's forensic team. He checked his watch and was amazed to see it was seven twenty — more than twelve hours since he had eaten, and then only a half slice of toast. He checked that the box had been dusted for fingerprints then called for someone to deliver it, along with the key, to the forensics' lab before punching

Charlton's home number into his phone. He knew it was a big call to expect Charlie, as he was affectionately known to one and all, to turn out at night — even if it was urgent. But this was Charlie, and it wouldn't be the first time he had put himself out for Sam.

'On a scale of one to ten, how urgent?' asked Charlie, when he had signaled Laura to turn down the volume on the television.

'Twelve,' Sam said.

'OK,' Charlie sighed. 'The telly's rubbish, anyway. I'll meet you at the lab in,' he checked his watch ' . . . in an hour?'

'Done,' said Sam. 'I owe you one.'

'Well, mine's a pint,' Charlie said.

Sam laughed. 'That's a deal.'

Bacon rolls and pasties were the only hot offerings on the canteen menu at that time of night. Sam selected a pasty, and went to the machine to pour himself a mug of what passed for coffee at the Truro station. A couple of uniformed constables were the only other diners and Sam nodded across to them as he bolted down the meal.

The forensic lab was in an ugly red brick building not far from the station and Charlie's car was in the car park.

'Sam. How are you doing?' Charlie raised a hand in greeting as Sam walked in. Charlie was already at his bench examining Bentine's box. 'This is a right little Chinese puzzle you've given us.' He pushed his spectacles up his nose. 'Take a seat,' he said, indicating the vacant stool. 'You're going to like this.'

Sam slid in next to him and Charlie said 'How are the family?'

'Fine.'

'Ah. I'll take that as 'not fine' then.'

Sam shrugged. 'I'm in Jack's bad books. We were going fishing last Saturday when all this business down at Borlase kicked off.'

Charlie shook his head. 'We never learn to put our families before the job, do we, Sam? And I don't know why because at the end of the day nothing is more important than family.'

This was sounding distinctly philosophical for Charlie and he smiled when he caught Sam's quizzical look. 'I know, I know. Who am I, twice divorced, to be handing out relationship advice? But this time it will be different.'

Sam's eyebrow arched. 'This time?'

Charlie's grin split his face. 'I'm getting married again in two weeks' time . . . you're invited.'

'You sly old dog. I didn't even know you were seeing anyone. Do I know her?'

'Probably. It's Laura Bennington, over at the museum.'

'Well, the plot thickens,' said Sam. 'I was with her a day or two ago when a couple of that artist, Lawrence Kemp's, paintings were vandalised. I don't remember her saying anything about an engagement.'

'It's all very low key at the moment, and we want to keep it that way until the big day. Anyway, enough about our sublime happiness. This little box you brought in is fascinating. Do you want to know about it?'

'I want to open it.'

'Well, it's fortunate you didn't, or you would have destroyed all the evidence inside. Look here,' he drew Sam closer and demonstrated the sliding panel.

'Yes, I've seen that. But how do we get into the box when we don't know the combination?'

'Don't worry. We've worked that one out, but the point is the combination alone will not open the box, nor will the key. We need to use both together.' He looked up triumphantly. 'Now who would have thought of that.'

Who indeed, thought Sam? Only someone with a very devious mind.

Charlie turned the key a single ratchet and punched in a series of numbers. 'There's more,' he said raising his hand for Sam to be patient. 'One more turn.' The key clicked again and the lid sprang open. Sam stared into an empty box.

'What you're interested in is down here.' He reached into a drawer under the bench and produced a thick bundle of papers in a police evidence bag, which he tossed in front of them.

Sam stared at it. 'Andrew Charlton. I could kiss you.'

'I'd rather you saved that for the bride,' said Charlie, moving out of Sam's range, just in case. 'The wedding's at the Truro

Register Office, by the way, bring a friend.'

'How soon can I have this stuff?' Sam asked.

Charlie expelled air noisily. 'Give us a chance to check it over, Sam,' he sighed. 'How does tomorrow afternoon suit you?'

'I'd prefer the morning?' Sam's expression was pleading.

Charlie locked the papers back in his drawer. 'I like it when you grovel,' he said 'Where are we going for that pint?'

12

Loveday emerged from the shower, pulled on her white toweling robe and wound another towel around her wet hair. She frowned when she heard the knock on the door. Visitors were definitely not welcome on a Sunday morning. This was the pampering time she had promised herself all week. Maybe if she ignored it they would go away. She padded into the front room and peeked from behind the curtain, then cursed. Abbie Grainger's green Fiat was parked next to her own car. She had no choice but to let them in. The women looked surprised when she appeared in her dressing gown in the middle of the morning.

'Oh, we're intruding,' Abbie said, apologetically. 'We should have rung first. It's just that we were visiting St Michael's Mount,' she turned to indicate it, 'and it seemed rude not to call in.'

Kit looked uncomfortable, and to

Loveday's eyes, decidedly peaky. She said, 'This is obviously inconvenient. We shouldn't have landed on you like this. We'll go.'

'Actually,' Abbie cut in, 'there was another reason why we knocked on your door. Kit was feeling a bit faint.' Kit tried to shush her but Abbie ploughed on. 'It's quite a hike up to that castle. It's knocked all the puff out of her.' She cast a sympathetic glance at Kit and lowered her voice. 'She's a bit shaky on her feet at the moment.'

'I'm still here,' Kit snapped back, 'I *can* hear you.'

Loveday's brow creased in concern as she reached out to usher Kit into the cottage. The poor woman did look ill. Loveday was beginning to feel ashamed of her first instinct not to answer the door to them.

'Come through to the kitchen,' she said, leading the way and reaching to fill the kettle. 'It won't take me a minute to get dressed. Make yourselves at home.' She went to her room, pulled a pair of jeans from their hanger and was back dressed within two minutes, her long, dark hair brushed back into a damp ponytail.

Kit was at the sink filling a mug with water. 'It's for my pills,' she explained, 'I'll feel better once I've taken them.'

Loveday studied the thin, gaunt face and made a decision. 'My neighbour is a doctor. I think he should take a quick look at you. I'll be just a minute,' she called, heading for the door with the women's protests ringing in her ears.

'No problem. I'll just get my bag,' Adam said, when Cassie repeated Loveday's request. He appeared in bright yellow t-shirt and jeans and followed her at a brisk pace back to her cottage.

'This is Dr Trevillick,' Loveday said, 'I think you should let him check you over, Kit.'

Kit frowned, and snapped, 'I'm fine. I don't need a doctor.'

'Probably not,' Adam smiled, and Loveday could see why he was such a popular GP. 'But since I'm here — ?'

Kit nodded indifferently and Adam lifted her limp wrist and checked her pulse before putting a hand on her forehead.

'You're hot,' he said, frowning. 'I'll just take your temperature.'

The others watched in silence as he concluded his brief examination.

'You seem very run down, Miss . . . I'm sorry, I don't know your name.'

'It's Kit.' The voice was flat.

Adam studied her. 'Well, Kit. You really should be resting.'

'Quite right,' Abbie said. 'We'll drive back to the hotel and get you off to bed at once.' She turned to the others. 'I knew we should never have attempted to climb up there today. It's been too much for her.'

'I told you. I'm fine,' Kit raised a hand to quell any further discussion about her health. 'I've taken my pills, and now I'm fine.'

'Pills?' Adam queried. 'Can I see them?'

Kit produced a small brown bottle from her bag. 'I take them for my nerves.'

Adam examined the bottle and nodded before giving her an earnest look. 'I meant what I said about the rest. No more gadding about, not for a few days at least.'

Loveday had produced four mugs of instant coffee and handed round the milk and sugar.

'My fault. I confess,' Abbie held up her hands to emphasise her guilt. 'I wanted us to make the most of our time in Cornwall. Doing the round of sightseeing has been a way of taking our minds off . . . well, other things.'

Out of the corner of her eye Loveday saw Kit shudder. It was a reaction to that awful memory that Loveday knew only too well. It had been bad enough for her, but for Kit, who was already struggling to cope with the death of her sister, it must have been a living hell. No wonder the poor woman was strung out.

The scene at Borlase Cove once more flashed, unbidden, into her own mind. She was standing at the edge again, her hand clamped over her mouth, staring down at the horror below. Abbie was behind her, body stiff as a statue. Shock took some people like that. She could see

213

Ben, gently leading her away from the edge and back to the others. That's when Loveday had caught sight of Kit. Her eyes were wide, her expression full of horror. And then she collapsed. But had there been something else there, something Loveday initially missed in the trauma of that awful morning. Had there been fear in Kit Armitage's eyes?

Adam's voice cut into her thoughts.

'Is this your first time in Cornwall, ladies?'

Both women nodded.

'Not the best introduction to our beautiful county,' he said.

'That's why we stayed on,' Abbie said, quickly. 'We didn't want this terrible murder to be our lasting memory of Cornwall.'

Adam nodded. 'Good idea,' he grinned, putting his empty mug on the table. A thought struck him as he made for the door and he turned. 'Once you're feeling up to it, Miss . . . er . . . Kit, you might try a day's sailing. All that sea air in your lungs . . . ' he took a deep breath and Loveday knew he was picturing days out in his own little boat currently waiting across the road in the sailing club compound for its next outing.

'We wouldn't know one end of a boat from the other,' Abbie said.

'I was thinking of a sail down the Fal on one of the tourist boats,' Adam said, 'if they're still sailing at this time of year.' He picked up his bag and with a little bow to the three of them was out of the door and away.

'Nice man,' Kit mumbled, in one of her rare unprompted utterances. 'I think we should be going now, Abbie. We've already intruded too much on Loveday's day off.'

This was new too. Kit taking control. It was good to see her asserting herself for once. Loveday wondered just how strong the little nerve pills Kit was popping actually were. She followed them out to their car and waved them off as they made a noisy exit up the drive and out onto the Marazion seafront. Her plans for a lazy day finishing the library book that was now overdue had been interrupted. Loveday changed into the tracksuit she wore for running and pulled on her old trainers. The tide was out and she headed for the beach.

It was the reappearance of the women that had got her thinking. Loveday had tried to recall something that at the time she'd thought was strange. Now she remembered what it was. When she told them one of her friends had been taken in for questioning, Abbie had said, 'They surely don't think *he* could have done this?' She'd said 'he', but Loveday was certain she'd made no mention of her friend being male. Had that been a reasonable assumption on Abbie's part? She frowned. She was getting paranoid.

Loveday got to work early next morning and was typing up an interview she had recorded earlier when her mobile rang. She picked it up.

'Loveday? It's Lawrence. I'm at the museum, and I need you to come over right now, if you can.'

The urgency in his voice set alarm bells clanging in Loveday's head. She'd never heard him so agitated. 'What's wrong, Lawrence? What's happened?'

'There's something I need you to see. It's important, Loveday. Can you come now?'

She could see her diary lying open at the page where she had scribbled in details of the telephone interview she'd arranged in half-an-hour's time with a couple who had just opened a new bakery in Fowey.

'Well, I'm a bit pushed this morning. Can it wait an hour or so?'

'Not really. I need you to see this.'

'I have to be back here within the hour.'

'Yes, that's fine. Just get over here, can you?'

She glanced up at Keri who was mouthing that she should go. 'I'll ring the people in Fowey and tell them you'll be calling a bit later than planned.'

Loveday smiled her thanks and reached for her jacket. Truro's city centre was always busy and today was no exception, even though the lunchtime rush was still a long way off. Her heels clicked on the uneven pavement as she turned out of Lemon Street and, dodging traffic and shoppers, crossed Boscawn Street. A few minutes later was running up the museum steps. Lawrence was waiting with Laura at the reception desk and both smiled a greeting. 'Well?' Loveday asked, arching an eyebrow at him.

'In the gallery upstairs,' he said, taking her arm and hurrying her through the main exhibition hall, past the displays of Cornish artifacts in their glass cases. She struggled to keep pace with him as he bounded up the stairs to the upper gallery where his vandalised paintings had hung. She followed him in, narrowing her eyes to adjust to the darker surroundings. Spotlights picked out the various paintings, showing the work of the local artists to best advantage. Lawrence stopped before his picture of Borlase Cliffs.

Loveday gasped. 'Your painting, Lawrence! You've managed to restore it.'

'No, this is another one that I painted weeks earlier, but it was so similar to the damaged ones that the museum agreed to hang it.'

'It's wonderful, Lawrence. Is that what you wanted me to see? I thought the building was on fire.'

But he wasn't listening. 'I thought the paintings were more or less identical,' he said. 'It was only when I had hung this one that I remembered.'

'Remembered what?'

'The figure. Don't you see? There was a figure in the other picture . . . somebody standing at the cliff edge. It looked kind of poignant somehow, so I painted him in. Well, *it*, I couldn't tell if it was a man or a woman.'

'I'm sorry, Lawrence.' Loveday spread her hands in a gesture that showed she was mystified. 'I don't understand. What's your point?'

'Don't you see? This could be why the painting was destroyed. Maybe it wasn't the actual picture the vandal wanted to deface — just that figure.'

Loveday shrugged. 'I still don't see.'

'I painted that a couple of weeks before Bentine's murder.' He looked at Loveday, his eyes glowing with excitement. 'What if my figure was the murderer . . . checking out the location . . . planning his crime?'

Loveday's eyes widened. 'Where has all this come from? Come on, Lawrence. It's all a bit far fetched.'

'I know, but just think. What if that figure was the murderer, and he recognised himself in my painting?' He searched Loveday's face for any sign of her believing his theory. 'That would explain why my painting was attacked. The killer was destroying the evidence!'

Loveday let out long, slow breath. 'It stretches credulity a bit, don't you think? I mean, could this figure actually be identified? You said you couldn't tell if it was a man or a woman. And anyway, why would it matter?'

'It might matter. That person was on the cliffs a few weeks before Paul Bentine's body was found down there.' He stopped to look at her. 'I know it's a long shot, but what if that actually was the killer, and he or she was out there doing some kind of recce? How shocked they would have been if they had visited the gallery, seen my painting and recognised himself — or herself?'

A tiny knot of excitement began to form in Loveday's own stomach. Lawrence's theory was so far fetched to be bordering on the ludicrous, but what if he was right? On the other hand, the painting had been destroyed, so any evidence, however slight, was also gone.

'I know what you're thinking: that this is all in my mind and that I have no proof, but there's this,' he pulled a dog-eared sketchbook from his satchel.

'I always start a painting by making a sketch of the subject.' He flipped over the pages and turned the book towards Loveday. 'You see,' he said, pointing to the charcoal image. 'That's him.'

Loveday looked down at the familiar image of the mine stack at Borlase and her eye was drawn to the edge of the drawing and the distant figure outlined against the emptiness of the sky. There was an outline of a jacket, trousers . . . it could have been anybody.

'Is this your proof, Lawrence?' she asked, her voice rising in disbelief.

'I know it's not much, but the figure in the painting would surely have been much more recognisable to the person involved. Look at the cap,' he insisted, pointing. 'Who wears anything like that anymore?'

Loveday shrugged. She could make out only the merest outline of a hat.

'I know it's not very clear here, but it was better in the painting, because I remembered it.'

'Could you draw it again, Lawrence, just what you remember?'

He took a pencil from the top pocket of his jacket and began to sketch.

Loveday looked at the finished sketch. She had no idea how it would help. She could imagine Inspector Kitto's disbelieving look if she produced this 'evidence', but she couldn't afford to care about that. This was about Lawrence and she was determined to do all she could to help him. He was grinning at her now.

'Ok, Loveday. I know you think I've lost my marbles.' The light in his blue eyes was still confident. 'But you have to look at this with an artist's eye — and there was something about the body language of that person that made me paint him into the picture,' he shrugged. 'That's all I can say. Call it instinct.'

Loveday still looked unconvinced as Lawrence went on, 'The way a person stands, walks, turns, holds his head, the slope of a shoulder — all the clues are there. It's how we recognise our family and friends if we don't actually see their faces. Artists capture that all the time.'

'I'm trying to understand, Lawrence, really I am.'

He held her stare. 'I think this person,' he jabbed a finger at the crude sketch, 'recognised themselves, and if he or she was on the cliffs that day, checking things out . . . ' He left the sentence unfinished.

'Just a minute, Lawrence.' Her eyes fell to the sketch. 'I can't believe you really think that this,' she jabbed a finger at it, 'is the murderer.'

'That's exactly what I'm suggesting. It would explain why my perfectly innocent painting was destroyed. Don't tell me the police aren't considering a connection?' He took her hand. 'Will you help me Loveday? All this would sound so much better coming from you. Let's face it, they're not likely to believe *me*. They'll probably think I've made the whole thing up.'

He left her no choice. 'You know I'll

help,' she said, smiling. But after the fuss about the keys for the Blue Lady, she guessed she wasn't at the top of Sam Kitto's list of favourite people.

★ ★ ★

Will and Amanda exchanged knowing looks when Sam strode back into the office, his face like fury. 'He's had a rollicking,' said Will, throwing down the pen he was using to check through the reports for the umpteenth time. 'What do they bloody expect? Do they think we've been sitting on our backsides doing nothing for the past week?'

'Of course they do,' Amanda grimaced. 'It's them upstairs, and us. We do the work, and they do the complaining.'

'Aye, but they're happy enough to take the credit when we do pull rabbits out of the hat,' Will said, watching Sam's back retreat into his office.

'We should have known the Bentines had a boat, though,' Amanda said, quietly.

Will shrugged. 'Well, we didn't know, and we all need to take responsibility for that. It's not the boss's fault, but he's the one getting the kicking.'

'Rank has its privileges,' Amanda grinned, and Will threw an empty coffee carton at her before striding to the window to scowl down at the little cluster of journalists gathered outside. 'And now we've got this lot breathing down our necks. It's all we need.'

The tabloids in particular were having a field day with the story, producing one sensational, and Will thought, outrageous front page after another. The nature of Bentine's demise had caught the collective imagination of a certain section of the press and it was not letting go. But they hadn't yet found out about the papers he and Sam had uncovered on the boat. This was a much more high profile list of characters than the local names they'd discovered on the computer stick. These people were big time, high ranking movers and shakers. Two of them were High Court judges; there was a junior cabinet minister, bankers, city bosses — and the owner of a High Street fashion chain who, if Bentine's dossier was to be believed, was funding his business from his dealings with a crime syndicate.

Any of these people could have killed Bentine, or at least put out a contract on him, Sam told the troops at the early morning briefing. The dossier was a potential bombshell — one for the Met, or maybe even MI5. But he was determined that his team, working as discreetly as possible, should check out alibis for some of the main characters before the information was out of their hands.

Sam's head appeared round his office door as he beckoned Will and Amanda. He was by the window when they came in, his arms folded over his grey suit jacket, his expression grim. 'Sit down.'

They did, but Sam remained standing.

'OK. What've we got? You first, Will. What did the checks throw up?'

Will blew out his cheeks. 'The one we have to call X was out of the country at the time. Y has a watertight alibi. He was with his mistress.' He shook his head. 'They never learn.'

'What about the banker?'

Will shrugged. 'Same thing. He has an alibi.'

'What about these, then?' Sam slid the pair of sinister, threatening notes they had found in Bentine's box, across the desk.

Will shrugged. 'We're still working on them.'

'Well work harder,' Sam snapped, turning to Amanda. 'What about our artist friend, Kemp? He knows more than he's saying. I'm sure of it.'

'I agree, boss,' Amanda said. 'Want me to bring him in again?'

Sam shook his head. 'Not yet, but keep digging.'

The phone rang and Sam snatched at it and barked 'Yes?'

'Oh dear,' said the rich Cornish burr of Andrew Charlesworth. 'Bad time?'

'Sorry, Charlie, didn't mean to snap.' He nodded to the others to leave. The anger from having been made to feel like a naughty schoolboy in the Superintendent's office earlier was still simmering. He had been given an ultimatum. 'Forty-eight hours, Sam. That's the best I can do. If you can't shift this case on in that time

227

then I'll be taking charge of the investigation myself.' Superintendent Harry Bolger had spread his hands in a helpless gesture. 'It's not up to me, you know that.' He flicked a thumb at the ceiling. 'It's the top brass . . . never satisfied until the line's drawn under every bloody case.'

But Sam knew Harry Bolger was just itching to get his hands on this one.

'Sorry, Charlie. Bad day. What can I do for you?'

'I heard something over lunch that might interest you. It might be nothing, but there was a bit of a drama at the museum earlier concerning that artist chap you had in for questioning.'

'Lawrence Kemp?' Sam sat up.

'That's the one, something to do with that painting that got trashed.'

'What about it Charlie?'

'Don't know, really, but according to Laura, he got very excited and insisted on calling some journalist he knows.'

'Not Loveday Ross?' Sam's jaw tightened. Everywhere he turned it seemed that Loveday was there before him. She was beginning to set his teeth on edge.

'That's the name. She's a friend of Laura's actually. Anyway, she came round and there were some heated discussions about the painting. It might be something, Sam. I don't know. Anyway, I'll leave you to it. By the way, have you decided about the wedding yet?'

'Wedding?'

'You've forgotten, you bugger! The wedding . . . my wedding? Ring any bells?'

'Oh yes; no I hadn't forgotten,' Sam lied. 'I'll be there.'

'You better be. You're one of the witnesses.'

'I'll be there, Charlie. Don't worry.' But his mind was on Loveday Ross. What was she up to now?

13

Loveday's head was spinning as she walked back to her office. Even if Lawrence's theory that he might have captured Bentine's killer on canvas was a cockeyed one, surely it must prove his innocence? No guilty man would come up with a story like that and expect to be taken seriously would he? The streets were busier now and she bit her lip as she hurried on, trying to make sense of what she'd just heard. Surely it proved he'd had nothing to do with Bentine's murder? For all his artistic talent, surely Lawrence wasn't devious enough to make up a story like that. She shook her head, oblivious to the looks she was attracting from passing strangers, angry now with herself for harbouring even a second's doubt. No, she'd been right all along, and Lawrence had absolutely nothing to do with this business.

As she reached the end of River Street

something made her look back and she caught sight of a figure, head bowed, turning quickly away from her. She stopped, frowning. She hadn't seen the face, but there was something . . . the body language Lawrence had been talking about perhaps. Then she knew what it was she had recognised. It was the cap, so similar to Lawrence's drawing in her bag. The figure was too far away to be sure if it was a man or woman, but judging by the height and dress, Loveday thought it was a man. On impulse she hurried after him, followed as he turned along one of the narrow passages between the shops and into busy King Street. He was moving quickly, extending the gap between them. Did he know he was being followed? By the time she had reached the Coinage Hall she'd lost him. She stopped, staring back through the crowds. What was she doing? Her imagination was playing tricks on her. She'd have to get a grip.

Head down, checking her watch, Loveday was on the point of turning back to her office when she caught sight of a face she really did recognise. 'Inspector

Kitto,' she called across the street. 'I was coming to see you.'

'About what?' he called back, striding towards her.

The pavement was crowded and they were beginning to attract attention. 'We can't talk here. Can we go back to the police station?'

'I've a better idea,' Sam said, steering her towards the pub.

Loveday found an empty table up at the back while Sam went to the bar to order their drinks — a pint of ale for him and a glass of house white for her. 'I've ordered a couple of sandwiches,' he said. 'Hope you like cheese and pickle.

'Well?' He put down their drinks and slid into the bench seat opposite her. 'What do you have to tell me?'

Loveday bit her lip, unsure where to start. She looked up and found him watching her. She suddenly felt embarrassed. He was expecting her to reveal some vital piece of information, but what did she have?

He raised an eyebrow, waiting for her to begin.

'Ok, maybe it's nothing,' she started. 'I promised Lawrence I would pass this on.' Loveday spent the next five minutes recounting Lawrence's theory about the figure he had painted into his vandalised picture of the Borlase cliff top.

Sam studied her as she spoke, but his expression remained impassive. Charlie had fired his interest when he'd told him about the museum incident. It could have been the breakthrough they needed. But this was nothing more than fanciful, the product of an overactive imagination. He'd been hoping for more.

Loveday saw his eyebrows descend into a frown as she spoke. Her story wasn't impressing him. Determined not to be put off, she carried on, 'OK, I know it sounds far fetched, but there could be something in it . . . couldn't there?'

Sam sighed and spread his hands, 'I'm sorry, Loveday, but I can see nothing of any consequence here.'

'Well, look at this,' Loveday pulled the sketch from her bag. 'Lawrence asked me to show you this.' She offered the sketchbook across the table and Sam took it and flicked through the pages.

'That's the one,' Loveday said, stopping him at the Borlase scene. She pointed.

'That's the figure he's talking about.'

Sam glanced at the pencil sketch and shrugged. 'Could be anybody,' he said, 'man or woman.'

'Well, yes . . . but if it really was the murderer, and he thought he could have been identified in the painting, then it might make sense of the vandalism, don't you think?' She paused to gauge his reaction. He wasn't buying any of it. 'All right, I can see what you're thinking.'

His eyes flickered over her and Loveday wondered if he was assessing her sanity, but she wasn't going to back down now. She jabbed a finger at Lawrence's sketch. 'Look more closely,' she ordered, pointing to the cap. 'It's a bit unusual, don't you think?'

Sam shrugged. 'It's a cap. What's unusual about it?'

The barman brought their sandwiches and left them on the table. Loveday sat back, waiting till he was out of earshot again. 'How many hats like that have you seen about Cornwall recently, Inspector? It's sixties retro . . . straight out of an old John Lennon movie.'

'If you say so,' he said. But he did take a second look and maybe she was right. The shape was distinctive.

Loveday's attention had shifted to the sandwiches. She lifted one and examined it suspiciously before biting into it. Cheese was not her favourite food, but it was sharp and tasty — and she was hungry.

Sam smiled to himself as he watched her attack the snack with gusto, before taking an elegant pinky to brush away the crumbs at the side of her mouth.

'Very nice,' she said, 'Thank you. I was starving.'

She pushed her plate away and glanced up at him. 'Still not convinced, are you Inspector?' She didn't wait for an answer. 'The thing is . . . I thought I saw that hat just before we bumped into each other.'

She met his eyes. 'You see, Lawrence has this theory about body language and how we all recognise the people we know, even if we don't actually see their faces.'

'Go on.'

'I know this is going to sound weird, but I think I recognised somebody earlier. It was just like Lawrence said, something about the slope of the shoulders, how he held his head.'

'So who was it?'

'That's just it. I'm not sure, but it was somebody I know. I'm sure of it, and he was wearing the hat. I tried to follow him, but he was too quick for me.' She shrugged. 'And then you appeared.'

Sam rolled his eyes.

'You think I've lost my marbles, don't you? You're probably right. It does sound crazy.'

'I didn't say that,' Sam sighed. 'It's far fetched, certainly, and, well, not very likely.' He ran a finger up the side of his glass and drew a line in the condensation. 'But we won't discount it.'

He wasn't in a position to discount anything at the moment . . . not even a cockeyed theory like this one. He emptied his glass and checked his watch.

'Yes I know. I have to get back too,' Loveday said, anticipating what he was going to say. 'But,' she grimaced, unsure if she should go on. Her suspicions about Magdalene would probably be received as even more far out, but she was here now, so she would tell him.

He raised an eyebrow, and Loveday noticed how intense his dark his eyes were.

'I'm not saying this is true, but . . . well, it's about Magdalene Bentine.'

Sam's shoulders squared. 'You have something to tell me about Mrs Bentine?'

'Well, yes, and no,' she hedged, wondering how wise she had been to start this. But now that she had, there was no going back. She straightened her back and looked directly at Kitto.

'I think she was having an affair with a vicar. The Rev Martin Foyle.' She sat back and waited for his reaction.

'You know this for a fact, do you?'

'Not exactly a fact, no, it's just a theory at the moment.'

Sam's brows furrowed and he gave her one of his dark looks. 'Another one of your theories, Miss Ross?'

'I know,' Loveday muttered, staring

into the dregs of her wine. 'I shouldn't have started this. Just forget I spoke.'

She stood up to leave, but Sam touched her arm. There was no sign of a smile, but his voice was less mocking. 'Why don't you sit down and finish your story?' he said.

'Loveday toyed with the stem of her glass. 'The affair is just a gut feeling.' She smiled up at him. 'But I can usually trust my instinct on these things. Someone rang Magdalene on her mobile the day Cassie and I were at her house — and she was pretty quick to cover it up . . . but not before I had seen the name that came up on the monitor. It was Martin.'

'If Mrs Bentine is having an affair with her vicar then they won't want to be shouting about it,' said Sam.

'Exactly. But if her husband found out and threatened to expose them . . . ' Loveday's unfinished sentence ended in a shrug.

And for the first time that day, Sam did smile. It crinkled the comers of his eyes and made them twinkle.

'You think Magdalene and the vicar

killed Paul Bentine to shut him up?' he said.

Loveday frowned. 'Not necessarily . . . but they could have.'

Sam shook his head, but he was still grinning. 'I'll give you this much, Loveday Ross. You're persistent.'

'I'm a journalist,' she said. 'Persistence in my profession is an admirable quality.'

It was the wrong thing to say. Sam didn't need reminding that she was a journalist. His mood changed instantly. Just for a few seconds she could have believed they were friends. But the policeman was back. He stood up.

'Sorry. I really do have to get back to the station. It was an interesting conversation, Miss Ross.' He didn't say 'We should do it again some time.'

Loveday watched him leave, ducking his head to exit the low door. She drained her glass and gathered up her things.

Sam didn't go back to the office. Outside in the street he turned the other way and headed, instead, for the museum. Whatever had been going on there he would have to find out for himself. He knew Laura Bennington only slightly, but as he was soon to be a witness at her and Charlie's wedding, it would do no harm to renew the acquaintance

There was no sign of her as he walked into the reception area. Until recently the space had been wasted, used only to display a few posters. Now it housed a cafeteria, whose coffee and home baking was popular with tourists and locals alike. His nose twitched at the coffee aromas. A woman, who Sam estimated to be in her late forties, was sitting at the reception desk. She lifted her head and smiled as he approached. He produced his warrant card and asked for Laura.

The woman's previous composure slipped for an instant and she looked flustered. Why did people feel uneasy around the police? She lifted the phone and told the person at the other end that he was waiting.

'Miss Bennington will be right down,' she said.

Laura appeared on cue. 'Inspector Kitto . . . Sam,' she smiled, extending her hand in greeting. She looked over at the coffee area. 'Can I get you a drink?'

Sam nodded his thanks and Laura signaled to the woman at the coffee machine, who was settling back to hang on to their every word.

They sat at a table out of earshot. 'How can I help?'

'I understand there was some kind of incident this morning . . . concerning Lawrence Kemp and his painting?'

'Ah. I see. Andrew told you.'

Sam had to think for a moment to figure out who Andrew was. Like the others at the station, he only knew him as Charlie. Their coffees arrived and they thanked the assistant. Laura stirred her cup, her expression thoughtful. 'Yes,' she said quietly, 'he got quite excited about something in the painting. To be honest. I didn't really understand what he was talking about. Loveday could probably tell you more.' She looked up at him. 'I'm sorry. Loveday Ross . . . she's a friend of his. Lawrence called her.'

Sam nodded. 'I know Miss Ross.' He drained his cup. 'In fact, I've already spoken to her.'

'You'll know more than me then,' Laura said.

As she spoke Sam was looking round the area. He nodded towards the CCTV cameras. He'd spotted them as soon as he walked into the museum.

'Do you keep all the footage?'

'Only for a few weeks, then we record over it.' She smiled. 'Budgets, you know.'

'But you would still have the footage for the day Kemp's painting was vandalised?'

She shook her head. 'The other officers asked that at the time. We don't have cameras covering the local artists' exhibitions. So there's nothing of the actual vandalism on tape I'm afraid.'

His team had investigated the attack on Kemp's painting, but at the time they had been more interested in the artist who had painted it. He remembered Amanda Fox reporting that there was no CCTV footage covering the section of the museum where the local artists' work was displayed. It had been reasoned, she explained, that the museum, being short of cash, had concentrated their resources on the areas displaying the irreplaceable and valuable artifacts. Though no doubt the works of some of these local artists would also merit that description in years to come.

He turned his attention back to Laura. 'But you would have a record of who came into the museum that day?'

Laura looked surprised. 'Why, yes. Could that help?'

'It might,' said Sam. 'Perhaps you could dig it out for me.'

The tapes were duly recovered and put into a thick brown envelope, which Sam took back to headquarters. He set Amanda on the task of going through the footage.

'What am I looking for?' she asked, brows knitted.

'If I knew that then the case would solve itself.'

Amanda shot him a look, and he realised he had spoken more sharply than he'd intended.

'Well I don't know, do I?' he said. 'But there might be something. See if you can recognise any of the visitors.'

It wasn't often he had to explain himself to Amanda. It was a sign of how frustrated his team was becoming. More than a week, and they were still no closer to finding Bentine's killer.

It was just over an hour before Amanda came back to him and he could see by her face that she had found something.

'It might be nothing, boss, but I think you should have a look at this.'

Sam followed her back to the main office, to the computer screen where she had paused the video. She clicked the picture back into motion and saw her senior officer's jaw tighten before a slow smile spread across his face.

'Well done Detective Constable Fox,' he said. 'Now come with me, we have a visit to make.'

Loveday walked slowly back to the office after Sam left her at the pub. She had to think, and she could best do that calmly at her cottage in Marazion. Telling Keri she would spend the rest of the day working from home, she collected her things and headed off.

Cassie's door opened when she heard

her friend's car approaching and she rushed out to meet her. 'Come in,' she called, her eyes shining. 'You won't believe this.'

The old oak table in the Trevellick's comfortably untidy front room was strewn with printouts of newspaper cuttings. Cassie selected one and handed it to Loveday. 'Recognise anyone?' Her eyes glittered with excitement. 'The name's different, but I'm right, aren't I?'

Loveday stared at the black and white image. What she saw didn't make any sense. 'This has to be wrong,' she said.

Adam came and put his arm around Cassie. 'There's no mistake, Loveday,' he said, quietly. 'Take a closer look.'

She did, but she still couldn't believe what she was seeing.

'You have to tell the police about this,' Adam said. 'Ring Inspector Kitto.'

Loveday's brow wrinkled as she stared at the paper, trying to work out what this new information could mean. One thing was sure — someone had a lot of explaining to do!

Assuring her friends that she would call Sam, she let herself in the back door of her cottage and dumped her things on the kitchen table. She'd noticed some post on the mat at the front door and went to the narrow hall to pick it up.

14

There were three letters, one obviously a bill, another was a circular, and she tossed them aside. The third envelope was hand-written. She picked it up and frowned at the odd way it was addressed.

'*Miss Loveday Ross, the Cottage at the Doctor s House, Marazion.*' It had a local postmark. Curious, she turned it over looking for clues to the sender, but there were none, so she opened it. Her mouth dropped as she read the first words.

'*Dear Loveday,*

'*I killed Paul Bentine, but then I think you already knew that. I'm coming clean now because I don't know how much longer I can keep up the clueless little wimp act. You saw through that too, Loveday, didn't you?*

'*But don't feel bad about it because Bentine deserved to die. I was just the lucky one who got to him first.*

'It was easy for me because I've done it before. I don't like bullies. My Barry was a bully. Now he's dead. I stuck a knife in him.

'Bentine was my brief back then. He said if I pleaded guilty he could get me off on diminished responsibility, or something like that. But he was a rubbish lawyer and I got seven years. So you can see why he had to die, can't you?'

Loveday's hand was over her mouth, her heart hammering as she read on.

'Abbie was the perfect cover — the posh, bossy one that everybody thought was in charge. It suited me to go on playing the part of poor, downtrodden Kit.

Not even Abbie suspected I knew how to handle a boat. She believed me when I told her I went for long, solitary walks. She'd no idea about the car, or the boat and trailer I had hidden in a lock up near here. But there's a look in her eye now that makes me think she's getting suspicious. I can't let her live if she knows about me. You can understand that, can't you, Loveday?'

There was no signature

Loveday dropped the letter and the pages scattered across the kitchen table. It was what Cassie had suspected when she'd spotted Kit's picture with the report of her trial . . . but to see an account written down so graphically, admitting she had killed Paul Bentine as well as her husband, was chilling.

Why hadn't she gone to the police when she had the chance? Abbie's life was now in danger, and it was all her fault! Her mind did an instant replay of the scene in her friends' cottage. Once again she was scanning Cassie's printout of the newspaper cutting, with the headline screaming out at her — 'Killer Wife Gets Seven Years.'

It was a report of Jane Smith, alias Kit Armitage's trial for the murder of her husband, Barry Smith. The prosecution alleged that she had premeditatedly killed her husband in cold blood by ramming a kitchen knife into his stomach. Smith had pleaded guilty to murder. Her solicitor told the jury that Barry Smith had engineered his own death, taunting his wife and urging her to kill him. He explained the man was a manic-depressive who had, on numerous occasions, beaten his wife. He told the jury that Smith had previously miscarried a baby after her husband assaulted her, and described other previous assaults. But Jane Smith was still convicted of murder and jailed for seven years.

She had to contact Sam. Poor Kit was obviously deranged . . . and now she was going to kill Abbie! Sam had to see this letter. She glanced at her watch. It was almost three o'clock. Would Sam be in the office? She chewed her lip anxiously as the dialing tone connected and the phone rang out at the police headquarters in Truro. But Sam wasn't there. He'd gone off somewhere with Will and Amanda.

She ran a hand through her hair, unsure what to do next. Then she remembered Sam had called her looking for Cassie. His mobile number would still be in her phone. She found it.

'Loveday? What's wrong?' He sounded anxious.

'This is all my fault,' she gasped. 'I should have told you before.' Her words were coming out in a garble. 'Kit Armitage killed Bentine . . . and now she's going to kill Abbie.'

'Loveday. Calm down. Just tell me quietly what all this is about.'

In a jerky voice, Loveday read out Kit's letter. She heard Sam's shocked intake of breath.

'Christ!' he said. 'Where are you now, at home? OK. Don't move from there. I'll send someone round to collect the letter . . . and don't touch it again, Loveday, it's evidence now.'

She watched the seconds tick by on the clock above the fireplace. Patience wasn't her strong point. She eyed the letter with unease as though the pages might spontaneously combust before her eyes. She didn't want it in her cottage.

If Sam had instructed the local police to pick it up then they should be here in minutes, but if it was to be one of his investigation team from Truro then who knows how long it would take them to get to Marazion?

Her mobile rang and she grabbed it. The number was not familiar, but the voice was. She froze. 'Abbie?'

'Oh, Loveday. Thank god I've found you. It's Kit. She went out walking this morning and hasn't come back. I'm really worried about her.' She paused, 'She said something about the cliff path near here, but it's been raining and, well, it'll be dangerous out there.' Her words were coming in gulps as though she was fighting for breath. 'Can you come, Loveday . . . at once?'

The hammering in Loveday's chest was her heart. Kit's letter was on the table. She could see the words from here . . . *'I can't let her live if she knows about me'*.

'Are you all right, Abbie? Where are you?'

'I'm in the car park at the Miners' Lamp. I've called the emergency services.'

'Well stay there until they arrive. Don't leave the car park. Do you hear me, Abbie? Don't attempt to go on the cliffs by yourself.'

Loveday squinted up the drive, but there was still no sign of any police car. She was beginning to panic. What if Kit wasn't really missing? What if this was an elaborate hoax to entice Abbie onto the cliffs?

She couldn't wait any longer. 'I'll be right with you Abbie,' she called. 'Wait there for me.'

Grabbing her jacket from the peg behind the kitchen door, she stuffed her phone into the pocket and picked up the car keys before running to hammer on Cassie's back door.

Cassie came out, wiping wet hands on her apron. 'Heavens, Loveday. Where's the fire?'

'Haven't got time to explain,' Loveday said breathlessly. 'The police are on their way. The letter they want is on the kitchen table. Tell them I've gone to meet Abbie Grainger in the car park at the Miners' Lamp. I think she's in some kind of danger!' her words tailed off into the wind as she slammed the car door and sped away down the drive.

Cassie frowned. Loveday was always in such a hurry. She checked to make sure her friend had locked her back door. She hadn't. Cassie went in and saw the pages of a letter scattered over the table. If it had been private, then the pages would have been folded back into the envelope.

Her hand flew to her mouth as she read the words. 'Oh my god, Loveday. What have you got yourself into now?'

Loveday's grip was tight on the steering wheel as she sped along the seafront. If she could believe Kit's letter, then the woman truly was deranged. She knew it was reckless, rushing off like this, but Abbie's life could be at risk and if she waited for the police then it might be too late. Surely they wouldn't be far behind her?

The car park at the Miners' Lamp was crowded. The pub's lunch menu was popular. She spotted Abbie's familiar red jacket at once, but today the woman's face, devoid of its usual careful make-up, was drawn and grey. Her hair was disheveled and straggly, but she didn't seem to care. She waved and Loveday hurried to meet her, glancing back anxiously for any sign of a blue flashing light. The police couldn't be far away now, could they? Loveday focused all her concentration on staying calm.

'There's still no sign of her,' Abbie screeched, hurrying across the car park.

She pointed out across the fields, to where the breakers would be crashing onto the rocks at the foot of the cliffs. 'Kit's out there, somewhere. What if she's fallen and broken her leg . . . or worse?' She ran a hand over her tousled hair. 'I've been nearly frantic with worry.' She gripped Loveday's arm. 'We have to look for her.'

'That's not a good idea, Abbie. We should wait for help.' But her words were too late. Abbie had turned and was already running in the direction of the cliff path. She tore after her, trying to keep up. The weather was closing in and Loveday's eyes were stinging in the sharp wind. 'Stop, Abbie,' she yelled, but the woman was running like a creature possessed. Loveday's breath was coming in gasps. This was the same rough farm road that she and Lawrence had walked. Had that only been a few days ago? It felt like a lifetime ago now.

She shot another desperate look back towards the car park, but still the police were nowhere in sight.

At last, gasping for breath, she caught up with Abbie and grabbed her arm, making her stop. 'What makes you think Kit would have come out here?' she panted.

Abbie was sounding remarkably calm now. 'This is her favourite walk. It's the solitude. She loves the sound of the sea, the cliffs, all of that.'

The words in Kit's letter came back to her. '*She believed me when I told her I went for long, solitary walks. She'd no idea about the car, or the boat and trailer I had hidden in a lock up near here.*'

They had reached the exposed cliff top, where the wind was even stronger. Loveday could hear the thundering waves as they crashed into the caves below and wondered if the weather had been like this the night Bentine died. The shocking image of his body in the cove that had haunted her since that awful morning came surging back.

Where was Sam for heaven's sake? Surely he must be speeding to her at this very minute? Where the hell was he?

It was then that Loveday realised something was missing. She stopped to listen. There was no sound of a helicopter. From here she could see a wide expanse of ocean, and there was definitely no rescue helicopter in sight. Nor was there any sign of a lifeboat. Surely if Abbie had called the emergency services, as she had said, then they would be here, out there searching. But there was nothing. They were all alone!

She bit her lip and forced herself to take long breaths. She needed to take stock of the situation, try to work out what was going on. 'We should call the police again, or the coastguards.' But her words came out strangled.

Abbie's eyes narrowed, strands of hair were plastered across her face. 'Not yet,' she said, 'we might find her ourselves.'

Loveday kept her eyes on Abbie's back as she picked her way along the precarious cliff path. The first drops of rain were in the air, with more great sheets of it blowing across the sea. Then she saw it! The pink jacket was spread over the rocks below. It was Kit's jacket. Why was it here? Then Loveday froze, staring down in horror. Kit's body lay face down, suspended on a jagged rock above the surging foam. Her right hand flung out, as though in some desperate bid to save herself. She looked like a hideous broken doll.

'She's dead, isn't she?' Abbie's voice was chilling. 'I warned her not to come out here, but she was so stubborn.'

Loveday swung round to face her. Abbie was shaking her head, her eyes glittering, but there was no sign of shock; nothing of the horror Loveday felt at seeing poor Kit's broken body at the foot of the cliffs.

Abbie had known where to find Kit. She'd led her to the very spot. Loveday tried to push away the thoughts that were now crowding into her head. To the left of the footpath the ground had been disturbed. The earlier rain had made it muddy and the impressions of footprints could be clearly seen. Loveday had a fleeting image of the two women struggling. Maybe Kit hadn't been as tough as her letter suggested. She could see Abbie's strong hands on Kit's shoulders . . . one last push and . . .

She felt a touch on her arm and recoiled. 'Are you all right, Loveday?' It was Abbie. 'You've had a shock. We both have. We must be strong for each other now.'

An involuntary shudder swept through Loveday's body. Had she got this all wrong? She couldn't have misunderstood Kit's letter . . . if it was Kit's letter. But it had been typed. There hadn't even been a hand-written signature at the end. Why hadn't she been more suspicious? A chilling horror was beginning to seep into Loveday's bones. She drew back from the edge, but not before Abbie had noticed her glance at the spot where she had struggled with Kit more than an hour before.

'We need to get help,' Loveday said quickly, turning back, but Abbie caught her sleeve.

'You know, don't you?' Abbie said. The control in her voice was disturbing.

Loveday frowned. 'Know?'

'That Kit didn't fall.'

Loveday felt her blood run cold.

'Poor Kit . . . life just got too much for her. She suffered so badly from depression.' She turned to Loveday. 'Well, you saw that for yourself, that day at your house . . . '

Abbie was shaking her head. 'Her sister

dying like that was just too much for her.'

'You think she killed herself?' Loveday asked incredulously.

'I know she did. I was here.'

Loveday stared at her.

'I followed her out here, saw her getting off the bus, held back until she had got past the pub, then I pulled into the car park and went after her.'

She looked up into Loveday's eyes.

'She was standing on the edge, staring down. I called out and ran forward to grab her. But she was like a wild thing, screaming that she had murdered Bentine and had nothing to live for. We struggled and I desperately tried to keep a hold of her, but she just slipped away.'

Abbie was staring over the edge now to where Kit's body lay. 'Poor little Kit,' she said quietly, then 'we can't leave her down there on her own. I'll go for help.'

'I thought you had already called the police?' Loveday said.

'No . . . I don't think I said that. But I'll go now.'

But Loveday wasn't listening. She was staring at something glinting in the stubble just ahead. It was half embedded in the mud, where it had been trodden in. She bent to pick it up. It was a button, a cheap brass button with an embossed anchor on it. It was just like the ones on Kit's jacket. She held it out in the palm of her hand.

'But this was nowhere near the edge, Abbie. If you were telling the truth then Kit had been nowhere near this spot.'

Abbie swayed closer, her face contorted into a sneer. 'So my letter didn't fool you? You just don't know when to leave things be, do you Missie? Going around like some kind of cheap amateur detective. Don't think I haven't been on to you. But there is nothing you can prove, is there? So you might as well know. Yes, I killed Kit. She was becoming a liability.' Her lips curved in a grotesque grin. 'She was getting guilt trips about Bentine. But we had to do it. We both knew that. He thought he had got rid of me, but it was him we got rid of.'

She advanced on Loveday and made a grab for her. 'And you're going to join your little friend right now.'

Loveday ducked and she felt Abbie's hands brush her shoulders as she stumbled. Loveday edged back and tried to get off the path, but the gorse on the banks was slippery after the rain. Abbie grabbed at her ankles.

'Say your prayers, journalist woman,' she rasped, her breath coming in short gasps as Loveday struggled to free herself.

'There's another letter!' Loveday screamed, praying the lie would buy her more time. 'Kit wrote to the police, telling them everything.'

Abbie released her grip and stared wide eyed at Loveday.

'You're lying,' she hissed.

'It's true. The police have it! They're on their way here right now. They're coming for you, Abbie, so there is no point in killing me.'

'You're lying you bitch, you're lying.' Her face was contorted with rage as she moved closer. Loveday could feel the woman's breath on her cheek. She made a grab for Loveday's hair, but Loveday ducked out of reach and Abbie caught her collar. 'Why are you lying?' Her words came out in a shriek that was instantly torn away by the wind.

Loveday struck out, caught the other woman a sharp blow to her face. She seized her shoulders and forced her to the ground. Abbie tried to wriggle out of Loveday's grip. But she was going nowhere . . . not this time. Loveday put a knee between Abbie's shoulder blades and pinned her to the ground. Where the hell were the police?

'You're assaulting me. I'll have you charged,' the woman was screaming

'Yes, you know all about that, don't you Abbie . . . you being a lawyer, I mean. At least you were until Bentine got you struck off. I know, you see. I've read all about you.

'You drugged Paul Bentine and made poor Kit help take him to that beach. You pinned him down and left him to drown.' Loveday could see it all now.

Abbie's face contorted in rage. 'Yes!' she shrieked, but the word was swallowed by the thundering of the waves below. 'He deserved to die. He was evil.' She was still yelling.

Loveday looked down to where Kit's body lay. 'She didn't deserve it though, did she?'

That second of distraction was all Abbie needed. Her fury had empowered her. She threw back her arms, sending Loveday flying. Then she was on top of her, grabbing Loveday's arms and forcing her face into the ground. Loveday could taste the mud, feel the grit scratching her face.

'If you care so much about poor little Kit you can join her.'

Loveday struggled desperately to find a footing, a boulder where she could wedge her foot, but Abbie had the strength of a tiger and was forcing her over the edge. She was slipping. At any second she would plunge to the rocks below.

Suddenly there was a noise behind her, feet running and scuffling. Abbie released her grip slightly as she too heard the sounds. Then there was a scream. Was it her own scream or was it Abbie's? Loveday didn't know. Tears were coursing down her cheeks and strong hands were going round her shoulders, pulling her back, back from the edge.

Loveday felt herself being lifted from danger, strong arms holding her close as she buried her face in the familiar softness of the tweed. It was the smell of home, the smell of the Highlands. Her father had come to keep her safe . . .

But the voice didn't belong to her father. It was an angry voice and it was shouting at her. 'How could you be so stupid, Loveday? Two more seconds and you would have gone. You couldn't leave it to us? You just had to get involved, didn't you?'

The hands that had held her so tenderly a few seconds ago were now grasping her shoulders, forcing her to look up into Sam's angry face. He was shaking his head.

Loveday pulled free and Amanda appeared beside them. She touched Loveday's arm. 'Are you all right?' she asked, gently.

Loveday nodded.

'Take her home,' Sam growled.

Loveday felt sick and foolish. She just wanted to get out of there. She could feel her face was wet, but didn't know if it was tears or blood.

'I'll get somebody to follow with your car,' Amanda said, guiding Loveday to her own vehicle and settling her in the front passenger seat.

Sam's forehead creased into a frown as he watched Amanda lead Loveday away from the cliff path . . . away from the horror of Kit Armitage's sad, broken body down on the rocks. He shuddered. Loveday had been seconds from joining poor Kit. Why couldn't she have just stayed at home and let them deal with this? It was their job after all, not hers.

But he already knew the answer. She'd have done it for Kit. She would have believed there was a chance that she could have saved her. But saved her for what, the rest of her life in prison? Sam doubted if the ill-fated Kit would have thanked her for that.

He turned and moved towards the edge, to the spot where just a few minutes ago his heart had stopped. He had grabbed Abbie off Loveday and hurled the woman away. He'd picked Loveday up and cradled her. Did she realise she'd been inches from death? He'd been angry. He couldn't remember what he'd said to her, but he knew it was harsh. He wished now that he had dealt with the situation more calmly.

He'd already lost his lovely Victoria, now another woman he'd grown to care for had faced death. Sam stared down to where the waves crashed against the rocks and a shudder went through him. He was seeing Loveday's body down there, another broken doll, with all that lovely dark hair spread over the unforgiving rocks.

They'd handcuffed Abbie Grainger's hands behind her, and she was being led away, flanked by two burly PCs. Sam glanced back down again, lips compressed in a hard line. They had another body to recover.

Cassie had been watching for Loveday's car and rushed forward, arms outstretched when she saw the strange car pull into the drive. She put her arm around Loveday's shoulders and led her indoors. Cassie's kitchen was warm, but the heat had not yet penetrated Loveday's bones and she was shaking. Adam made a cursory examination and, satisfied that Loveday had suffered no broken bones or other serious injury, nodded his approval for Cassie to gently bathe the cuts and grazes on her hands and face. Then he left, appearing seconds later with a glass of brandy.

'Drink it,' he said. 'It will make you feel better.'

It was an order, and Loveday did as she was told, contorting her face into a grimace as the powerful spirit slid down her throat making a fire in her belly.

'All of it.' Adam insisted, standing over her until she had complied.

'There, that wasn't so bad, now,' he smiled, taking the glass from her.

She had stopped shaking

'Better?' Cassie asked, her expression full of concern.

Loveday nodded. 'Much.'

Adam left them to it. He knew he would just be in the way if he hung around. Cassie had a better chance than he did of getting Loveday talking. That was what she most needed to do now, to talk. Talking about the ordeal, getting it all out into the open, would lessen the trauma of the situation.

'I'm fine now, really I am,' she said when the door had clicked softly behind Adam.

'Feel up to talking about it?' Cassie's voice was gentle.

Loveday nodded, but she was powerless to stop the tears as she recounted what had happened to her since she left Cassie, calling instructions for her to call the police only an hour or so earlier. Was that all it had been? It seemed to Loveday like a lifetime ago.

In a tremulous voice she told Cassie about the horrors on the cliff top, about Kit's pitiful broken body on the rocks. She described her struggle with Abbie, and how she'd fought for her life on the edge of the cliff. She'd believed she was going to die, then the arms had come around her, scooping her to safety. She could hear the gentleness in Sam's voice; feel his breath in her hair, the familiar smell of the tweed jacket. Tears were coursing down her cheeks because suddenly the voice had become harsh, accusing.

'How could you be so stupid?' He'd yelled.

15

Loveday had been a good patient. She'd swallowed the sleeping pills Adam had given her the previous night and had slept till daylight. She woke to discover one of those golden September mornings, when the birds decide that maybe summer isn't quite over yet. She tried to get up, but her body ached. Slowly she raised her shoulders from the bed and swung her legs to the floor. The worst pain was across her shoulders and neck. She winced, remembering how Abbie had pinned back her arms, forcing her face into the grit. She imagined she could still taste it. Suddenly she was trembling violently. She lifted her chin forcing slow, calming breaths into her lungs. 'I can do this,' she told herself, easing off the bed and putting her feet on the floor.

She stood up gingerly, testing her legs. Her movements were stiff and jerky, but at least she could walk. She got to the bathroom and turned on the taps. A good hot soak would make a new woman of her. She took a soft white towel from the cupboard, and then shrank back in horror as she caught sight of herself in the mirror. There were livid, angry scratches all the way down her right cheek and bruises under both eyes that were beginning to turn purple. She steadied herself on the side of the bath and felt tears of despair roll down her cheeks.

The sound of the running water brought Loveday to her senses and she got to the taps just in time to prevent the bathwater spilling over. For twenty minutes she soaked in the lavender scented foam, trying not to think about what had happened, but that was impossible. She could see Abbie's face, contorted with rage and madness. She could feel Sam's arms around her, hear his voice, gentle and comforting. Then he'd got angry. Why had he got angry?

When she stepped out of the bath she could move more easily. Even her bruised face looked a little more acceptable, but maybe she was just getting used to it. At least she was alive. There had been a moment out there on the cliffs when she thought she would die. Then the arms came round her, his arms, and the voice in her hair was tender and caring. Had she imagined that part? But Sam Kitto's anger had been real enough. He'd called her stupid, told her she shouldn't have meddled in police business — and then dispatched her home with a woman constable. She wasn't sure now what had upset her most.

Loveday at first thought she must be imagining the clink of cups from her kitchen as she emerged from the bathroom, wrapped in the white bath towel. But she hadn't. Cassie was there.

'They say lots of sweet tea is good for a crisis,' she called, filling Loveday's cream ceramic teapot with boiling water from the kettle. 'How are you today?' Her eyes were full of sympathy as she came forward to touch her friend's arm.

Loveday threw out a warning hand. 'Don't touch me.' She attempted a lop-sided smile. 'Everything hurts.'

Cassie nodded, understanding, 'Poor love,' she said, lifting a lock of damp hair from Loveday's face. 'You have been through the wars, haven't you? Well you go off and get dressed and I'll get the tea going.'

'I don't deserve you, Cassie,' she called from the bedroom as she carefully pulled on her jeans and shrugged into a soft blue sweater. She'd brushed her hair back and quickly platted it in a single long rope. Not glamorous, she reflected as she gazed at her mirror image, but maybe an improvement? She was reminded of another time when she was ten and had crashed her bike with a force. Her face had been scratched and bleeding then too. She smiled. Her mother had been there to comfort her — just as Cassie was doing now.

But there had been no comfort from Inspector Sam. The more Loveday thought about it the more indignant she became. If it hadn't been for her, the police would still be trying to find Paul Bentine's killer. She had delivered that killer to them on a plate. But was Sam Kitto grateful? No! In fact, he'd been completely obnoxious.

The mobile phone on her bedside

cabinet suddenly burst into life. Loveday reached for it and smiled at the caller ID. 'My god, Loveday! Are you all right?' Merrick sounded shocked.

'I'm fine,' Loveday assured. 'Really I am.'

'Is there anything I can do? I can drive over.'

'No, really. I'm fine now, Merrick, honestly. Anyway. Cassie's here, and spoiling me rotten.'

'Well if you're sure. But I'll be over tomorrow, whether I'm invited or not.'

'Look forward to it,' Loveday grinned, putting the phone down. A warm feeling was beginning to spread through her. She had such lovely friends.

Cassie was holding a mug of tea out to her when she came back to the kitchen and she sat down gingerly, sipping the comforting drink. 'I was thinking of going for a wander along the beach this morning.'

'Do you think that's wise?' She winced at Loveday's bruises. 'You don't want to frighten the natives.'

'Oh, thanks a bunch. Do I really look that bad?'

Cassie bit her lip and tipped her head

to the side as she studied Loveday's face. 'Let's just say you won't be winning any bonnie baby competitions this week.'

Later, they walked together to the end of the drive, stopping to watch the rabbits nibbling contentedly on the lawn. It was strangely comforting to see them there. No matter what traumas happened around them, their simple, uncomplicated lives carried on as usual. The sound of an engine made them look up as a small boat, its outboard chugging noisily, moved from the pier in the direction of the island. The tide was going out. Soon the causeway would be exposed. Loveday crossed the road and gave a backward wave as she headed along the seafront.

Cassie turned back up the drive, having already decided the day was too good to waste just pottering around the house. The school was on a half-day holiday. She would pack a few sandwiches and drinks, toss a couple of plastic chairs in the back of the Land Rover, collect Sophie and Leo from school and drive to St Ives. As she reached the door the crunch of tyres on the gravel made her spin round. Her hand went up to shade her eyes from the bright sun. 'Inspector,' she said stiffly. 'If you're looking for Loveday, you've just missed her.'

'I don't suppose you know where she's gone?'

Cassie bristled. If what Loveday had told her about this man was right, there was no need for courtesy. 'Is that any business of yours, inspector?' she snapped. 'Hasn't Loveday done enough for you?'

Sam's eyebrows descended into a frown. He'd probably deserved that . . . and more.

'Is she OK?'

The man looked genuinely concerned and Cassie relented. 'She's fine. She's a tough girl, our Loveday.'

The shadow of a smile crossed Sam's face. 'I know,' he said, glancing at Loveday's car in the drive. 'She hasn't gone far then?'

Cassie laughed. 'You're not a detective for nothing, are you? She's gone for a walk along the beach.'

Sam cleared his throat and inspected his shoes.

'You can come in if you like,' Cassie said.

Half an hour, and two cups of coffee later, Sam was strolling along the sea-front, hoping to intercede with Loveday on her way back.

He felt ridiculously nervous. Apologies didn't come easily to him, and he suspected that he had quite a lot of apologising to do. He had no idea why he had behaved as he had on the cliff top. He'd no right to have been so angry with her — annoyed, perhaps. She had, after all, interfered in his investigation, but he had to admit that she had also helped. They might not have Geraldine Fielding in custody now, having eventually con-fessed to killing Bentine after an extended interview into the wee small hours, if it hadn't been for Loveday

But she had put herself in danger, and they didn't exactly encourage members of the public to that. But he knew that wasn't the reason why he'd got so mad. Against his better judgment he seemed to have developed feelings for the spirited Miss Ross.

He passed the local hotel and checked his watch. The bar wouldn't be open yet and he was already swimming in coffee, and besides, if he went inside he might miss her. He sat on a bench in the little garden beside the hotel and watched the water lap away from the causeway to the Mount.

It was a day to be out. He lost count of the people strolling, and in some cases running, on the beach, their trainers making imprints on the damp sand. Waders were pecking along the tidemark. They reminded Sam of the tin toys his grandfather had produced one day from his attic.

A lone figure stood on the beach also watching the scene. A child kicked a ball and the figure limped to retrieve it, a long dark rope of hair swinging over her shoulder. It was her! His heart gave an unexpected lurch and, just for an instant, he thought of leaving. But that was stupid. Cassie knew he was here. She'd certainly tell Loveday. And she would add cowardice to what she must already think was a long list of his inadequacies.

He headed back towards Loveday's cottage, knowing that further along the road there were various access points to the beach. That way he could get down to the sand and stroll towards her without giving the impression that he had been watching her from the hotel garden.

Loveday was deep in thought as she strolled. She was thinking of another beach, near her home on the Black Isle, outside Inverness, where she and her brothers, Hugh, and Brodie, had kicked a ball. Of course, she had been there on sufferance. What self-respecting school-boy would want to play footie with his sister — no matter how good she was.

'Always one for the rough and tumble, that's our Loveday,' her father had so often said, ruffling her long, streaming dark hair. She wished she was home in Scotland with her family now.

The irritated cry of a gull rang out overhead and she shielded her eyes to look up and watch it. A family strolled leisurely ahead of her, their little boy kicking a ball across the beach. It rolled towards her and she moved forward, the stiffness making her limp, to retrieve the ball and tossed it back to the laughing child.

She recognised the man immediately and stopped, hands on hips, as he approached.

Sam hadn't been prepared for the sight of Loveday's bruised face, and was overcome by a sudden rush of tenderness. His first instinct had been to reach out for her, as he had done on the cliff top. But Loveday misinterpreted his stare and an embarrassed flush crept up her neck. She cradled her face, hiding the bruises from him.

'Adam says it's all superficial. I just have to go around for a few days looking like Dracula's mother till it all heals up.'

'I'm sorry,' he said, not daring to touch her. 'I'm so sorry.'

She rubbed her arm. 'You were a bit rough,' she said. 'I was only trying to help.'

'You could have got yourself killed. In fact you nearly did. You should have left all that to us.'

'You weren't there.' Her shoulders rose in a slow shrug. 'Besides, I thought I could help Kit.'

The mention of her name brought back

the picture of her body down on the rocks and Loveday turned away as she struggled to fight back the threat of more tears. There'd be no crying in front of Inspector Sam Kitto.

'Look,' Sam said, screwing his eyes against the bright sun. 'Do you fancy a drink.'

Loveday shook her head. 'Can we just walk?'

He nodded and they turned and headed away from the town, where the beach became rockier.

'Is the Bentine case closed now?' Loveday asked. The wind had got up and she winced as it tugged at her sleeve.

'I don't think you should be out walking like this. You should be at home resting.'

'I'm not an invalid. Anyway, Adam says exercise will be good for me; stops the joints and muscles stiffening up.'

'Fine,' Sam shrugged. 'And yes, as far as the Bentine murder goes. Geraldine Fielding, which is Abbie Grainger's real name, eventually confessed late last night.' He looked at her. 'Of course, the letter helped.'

Loveday frowned, confused. 'I don't understand. Abbie wrote that letter herself. It was all lies.'

Sam smiled. 'I'm talking about the other letter, the one that was waiting for me when we got back to the station yesterday, the one Kit really did write.'

Loveday stared at him. 'But I told her that. I told Abbie out on the cliffs that Kit had written to the police confessing everything.' Her eyes widened. 'You mean it was actually true.'

Sam nodded, grinning. He pursed his lips as though considering something, then pulled a plastic police evidence bag from his pocket. 'This is strictly against the rules, but in view of everything that's happened I think you should see it.'

The bag contained two sheets of handwritten scrawl that had been inserted back to back for easier reading.

For Detective Inspector Sam Kitto
Dear Inspector,
I am writing to you because I don't know what else to do. She doesn't let me out of her sight, but she's sleeping

at the moment so I'm taking my chance to write this.

Her name isn't Abbie, by the way, it's Geraldine Fielding — and I'm Jane Smith — and we met in prison. She's a lawyer and Bentine fixed it so she would do a stretch in prison and get struck off their legal books. I don't know how to describe it, but she can't go back to being a lawyer again. She made up things in a court case — fabricating evidence the judge called it, and Bentine found out about it and he shopped her. So that's why she got put inside. I was there because I killed my husband. I couldn't take the beatings any longer, you see, so I took a knife to him. Paul Bentine was my lawyer and he told me I had to plead guilty to murder. He said the courts would be lenient, but they weren't, and I got sent down. So you see, Geraldine and I both had reasons to hate Bentine.

At the time I couldn't understand how somebody like her would want to pal around with me. I mean, look at us. She's so full of herself, smart dresser, big ideas — and me — well, I'm just me. I know you must think I'm pretty dim, but I really didn't see where it all was leading.

Anyway, we both got out of prison around the same time and Geraldine took this flat in London. She's got money. She'd been checking up on Bentine and discovered he had moved from Cambridge to Cornwall, so she tracked him down ... watched his house and everything. She worked out a way we could get even. It was all planned. We would make him suffer, as he had made us suffer. That's all it was to be. We would put the frighteners on him. At least that's all I thought we were going to do.

It was easy for her to work something out. I think she enjoyed it. She knows Cornwall, you see. She used to come down here for her holidays. And later, when she was grown up, she used to sail around these parts. She knows all about boats, Geraldine. She used to be in some sailing club in Southampton — that's where she comes from — a housing estate in Southampton. She doesn't know I know that. She likes people to think she is posh. But her mum told me when she came to visit one day.

Loveday shook her head in disbelief as she read on.

She found out where Bentine lived and we went to his house. Geraldine drugged him and we put him in the boot of her car then drove to a little cove where she kept the boat she'd hired. She'd even hired wet suits and we changed into them so we couldn't be recognised if anyone saw us. She had it all worked out. When Bentine came round she produced a gun. Believe me, inspector, I had no idea she had a gun.

It was dark by then and we all got into the boat. Bentine thought it was a windup and that Geraldine would release him, but she didn't. When we reached the cove she threatened to shoot him if he didn't do as he was told. He'd begun to get frightened. I was told to tie him down to the beach with some rope and pegs she had brought. I thought we would go off and then come back again when he was good and scared. I now know that it had been Geraldine's intention all along to kill him.

Loveday Ross might have guessed by now we only made friends with her because she was a journalist. Geraldine said she would be in a good position to get feedback from the police about how their investigation was going. I just wanted to get away from Cornwall, but Geraldine said we had to stay on. She said we had to make sure we weren't suspects. *She's obsessed with it.*

That's why she destroyed that picture in the museum at Truro — Oh yes, that was her.

Loveday's eyes widened. So Lawrence had been right after all. She looked up at Sam, and he nodded. She read on.

Geraldine had got it into her head that it was her in the picture. There was a blob, a splash of paint, but she insisted it was her and that she could be identified by it just because she'd *been out there on the cliffs checking out the area. Even if it was her, which I'm sure it wasn't. Nobody could have possibly recognised her. But she was paranoid about it. So we went back the next day. She even made me carry the can of spray paint in my bag.*

I feel better for writing this. It's a comfort to me that somebody else now knows what we did . . . what she did. Geraldine needs to be stopped. I truly believe she is mad.

I'm leaving this letter with the pub landlord and trusting that he will post it to you, as he has promised.

Jane.

'So she really did mean to kill him,' Loveday said, flatly, as she handed the letter back to him.

Sam nodded. 'No doubt about it.' He took a deep breath and shook his head. 'You were right about that, too. Apparently she knew the history of that old pub we met up in. The idea of condemning Paul Bentine to a terrifying death appealed to her.'

'Abbie must have been planning this for a long time.'

Sam nodded. 'From the moment she was sent down. She blamed Bentine for that and spent all of her prison sentence plotting her revenge.'

'What about Kit?'

'I think she was just in the wrong place at the wrong time. I don't believe Kit was ever all that bothered about taking revenge on Bentine. He might not have been one of the greatest lawyers, but the courts found Kit guilty and so she was sent down. She would never have thought of revenge if Abbie, or Geraldine, to call her by her real name, hadn't talked her into it.'

'So what happened when they left prison?'

'According to Geraldine, she got a flat in London. She had money so that was not a problem. Kit joined her when she was released a few months later. I don't suppose it was very difficult to discover where Bentine and Magdalene had moved to, although they did keep a much lower profile when they came down to Cornwall.'

Loveday nodded, her brow creased in

thought. 'My guess would be that he sold up in Cambridge to get away from people who wanted to get even with him. He was a blackmailer. But I suppose you knew that?'

They knew plenty about that. Paul Bentine had had another laptop, and it had been recovered from Abbie's room in the pub where the women had been staying. She'd admitted stealing it from his house and copying selected bits of information, in particular, Lawrence Kemp's name, onto a memory stick. It was the one they found later — as they had been meant to — in his desk drawer. But Loveday didn't need to know that, not yet. It would all come out in court.

'What about Lawrence's painting? Was Abbie/Geraldine, whatever her name is, was she really responsible for that as well?'

Sam nodded. 'Apparently.'

'Did she tell you why she did it?'

Sam cleared his throat. 'She saw Kemp's painting when she and Kit visited the museum, recognised the location and got some sort of fixation that she was the figure on the cliffs'

'So she went back and obliterated it?'

'Something like that.' He turned to look at Loveday. 'So you were on the ball there too.'

'Not me. That was all Lawrence's idea.' She shot him a mischievous glance. 'As I recall, you rubbished it.'

'That's right. Rub it in.'

Loveday laughed. 'If it's any consolation, I did too, at the time. I told Lawrence he was mad.'

A helicopter, crossing the sky like a giant dragonfly, droned high above them.

'It's on its way to the Scillies,' Loveday said, her voice, reflective. 'Do you know the Scillies, Inspector?'

'It was Sam a minute ago,' he said, watching her. 'And no, I don't know the Scillies.' He glanced around him. 'This place is good enough for me.'

They had stopped to look back and take in the wide sweep of the coastline. They could see Mousehole across the water, the sun glinting on the windows of its picturesque little cottages.

Loveday nodded. 'I run down here.' She took a deep breath, enjoying the sensation of the clean air filling her lungs.

'I can see why,' he said, narrowing his eyes as he scanned the horizon.

'Reminds me of home,' Loveday explained.

'Scotland?'

'Yes.'

'Which part?'

'The Black Isle. My parents run a pub there. It's just north of Inverness.'

'And is it?'

'What?'

'Black?'

Loveday laughed and her nose wrinkled. 'More like green, but they do say the soil is rich and black.' She looked at him. 'And before you ask, it's not an island either.'

'All very clear. Sounds like a place that has to be seen to be believed,' Sam said as his phone rang. He pulled it from his jacket pocket and flipped it open. 'My son,' he said. 'Do you mind?'

Loveday nodded and Sam strode across the beach, speaking into his phone. When he came back a few minutes later he was frowning. 'I promised to take him fishing when this case was wound up.' He grinned. 'He's pinning me down.'

'How old is he?'

'Jack's eleven and Maddie is eight.' He paused, as though deciding whether to give any more information. 'They live in Plymouth with their mother.'

She nodded, and then looking up saw that he had been watching her. 'You don't ask many questions — for a journalist, that is.'

'No,' she said quietly, 'Even journalists have days off.' 'And know when to keep quiet,' she added silently.

'Don't know about you, but I'm starving,' he said suddenly, springing up from the rock where they had been sitting and extending a hand to help Loveday to her feet.

'Me too,' she said, realising that it was actually true.

'I know just the place.'

Loveday's hand went to her face. 'I'm no fit sight for company.'

'You'll love where I've got in mind,' he said before hesitating and turning to face her. 'And just for the record, you look fine.'

They went back to Loveday's cottage to

collect his car and she noticed Cassie's Land Rover had gone. Sam followed her gaze.

'They've gone to St Ives. A picnic was mentioned.'

Loveday turned a surprised stare on him.

'I was invited in for coffee, earlier,' he explained as he followed her into the cottage. Her phone was flashing on the kitchen table where she had left it. Three missed calls — all from Lawrence.

'Go ahead,' Sam said, when she motioned silently that she would check them. She walked through to the sitting room, leaving Sam in the kitchen and pressed the answer button.

'Loveday! What the hell's been happening? Cassie said you'd been hurt. Are you all right?'

'Cassie told you?'

'I phoned her when I couldn't get hold of you. She thought I knew.'

'What did she tell you?'

'That you'd been hurt . . . and that the police have charged someone for Bentine's murder.'

293

'That's right. I know her. She's a lawyer who used to work with Bentine. Look Lawrence. I can't talk right now. Can I call you back?'

'When?'

'Tonight. I promise.'

Kemp! Damn it! Sam had forgotten about him. Loveday had told him she would be calling him that night. They were obviously in a relationship. He glanced round the room. She had her own life here, and he wasn't any part of it. Not that he wanted to be part of it, he tried to convince himself. He wasn't looking for a relationship. The only reason he had come here today was to apologise for his behaviour yesterday . . . but what had he to apologise for? Loveday Ross had only herself to blame if she got into trouble.

She came back into the kitchen. She'd brushed her hair and it was hanging loose now around her face, the dark strands against her bruised skin emphasising how fragile she looked.

He imagined Lawrence Kemp coming here, could see him making himself at home, pouring wine, taking ownership of the little cottage . . . taking ownership of her. He was suddenly angry and he wasn't sure why.

The painkillers Loveday had taken earlier in the day had long since worn off and she flinched as she moved across the room.

'Sore?' Sam asked.

Loveday grimaced. 'All my own fault.'

'I'll second that,' Sam said, his face serious.

Loveday looked up. 'And what's that supposed to mean?'

'You said it yourself, Loveday. Self-inflicted injuries.'

She shook her head and stared at him for an explanation. When none came, she said, 'Have I done something wrong?'

'Now let me see,' he said, eyes searching the ceiling. 'Journalist . . . meddling . . . troublesome. Are you getting my drift?'

Loveday opened her mouth to reply, but his raised hand silenced her.

'What I'm getting at is that this was a serious investigation and you did rather interfere.'

Loveday was shaking. 'You know what,' she said. 'Let's just forget about lunch. I've lost my appetite.'

Sam turned to speak but, shaking his head, thought better of it.

Loveday moved to the door and held it open. 'Goodbye, Inspector,' she said, slamming it shut behind him.

She watched, eyes narrowed, as his car retreated at speed up the drive, the tyres sending gravel flying in all directions. The man really was insufferable.

Loveday went to the fridge. The bottle of Australian Chardonnay was half full and she poured herself a glass and took it outside. The rabbits on the lawn scattered as she sat down on the peeling wooden bench beneath her window. Even they were deserting her. She took a gulp and felt the cold liquid flow down her throat. Somewhere inside she could feel it begin to relax her. She sipped the rest more slowly. The rabbits had come back, emerging gingerly from their hiding places under the shrubs that bordered the garden. Inside the cottage her phone was ringing. Loveday tried to ignore it, but eventually she went and picked it up.

'Me again,' Merrick said. 'Just checking up on you.'

'I've already got a mother, Merrick,' she sighed.

'Oh dear. Touchy today aren't we?'

'Am I?'

'Want to talk about it?'

'Hmm, no, not really . . . but thanks for your concern. I just need a bit of space right now, that's all.'

'Sure?'

'Yes, I'm fine. I'll be good as new in a day or two. You'll see.'

'Well I'm here if you need me. Oh, and I don't want to see you back in the office until you really are well enough. Got it?'

'Got it,' Loveday smiled into the phone. 'And thanks Merrick. I really do appreciate your concern.'

'OK. Take care.'

'You too.'

She put the phone down and wiped her face dry. The tears were just delayed reaction from yesterday's ordeal.

She'd forgotten her promise to ring Lawrence, so wasn't prepared for his call later that evening. She knew she had to speak to him. It was one final loose end she had to tie up. 'Sorry. I was just going to ring you,' she lied. It was only a tiny fib, but she wondered why she had bothered to make it. 'What exactly has Cassie told you?' she asked.

'She said this woman attacked you. God. Loveday! What happened? I feel this is all my fault. If I hadn't got you involved in my problems none of this would have happened.'

'Actually, Lawrence. You couldn't be more wrong. Somebody told me today that I just can't help meddling, poking my nose in.' She let out a long sigh. 'It's what journalists do, isn't it . . . interfere?'

'Are you sure you're OK? You're sounding funny.'

Loveday wondered how many times in a day she would have to tell people she was 'fine' before they actually started believing her.

'It's been a funny kind of day.'

'What happened, Loveday?'

Over the next 20 minutes Loveday filled in details of the past few days' events. Lawrence listened in silence until she had finished.

'Christ!' he said. 'She did all that? She really did have it in for Bentine. He wasn't a nice man, but nobody deserves ending up like that. What happens now?'

Loveday shrugged. 'Geraldine Fielding has been charged with Bentine's murder and I suppose if Sa . . . ' She was going to say Sam, but there were more detectives than him in the Devon and Cornwall Constabulary. 'If the police can get enough evidence, she might also be charged with Kit Armitage's murder, depending on what the post mortem results throw up.'

'So, are you saying we can put all this behind us now?' Lawrence asked.

'I suppose I am,' Loveday said. 'Case closed.'

16

'Why Monday?' Sam had asked. 'Only you, Charlie, would get married on a Monday.'

Arthur Charlton shrugged. 'It was a cancellation. Registrars are very busy people, apparently. Besides, it was either grabbing this slot or waiting until December.' He grinned. 'No contest.'

'Very smart, boss,' Amanda looked impressed as Sam strode into the office. Other faces lifted from their work and gave 'good morning' nods as he passed. Sam had exchanged his Harris Tweed jacket and brown slacks for the charcoal suit that spent most of its life hanging unworn in his wardrobe. He had added a soft grey silk tie, which, according to the looks he got, was acceptable wedding attire. It didn't stop him feeling uncomfortable though. He wasn't used to such formal clothes, but Charlie was a friend and Sam felt compelled to make an effort. It *was* his wedding day after all.

The stack of papers in Sam's inbox appeared to have grown in his absence over the weekend. He knew that sooner or later he would have to knuckle down and attend to them — but not today. So maybe, despite his dislike of weddings, it wasn't all bad.

The euphoria in the office at getting that confession from Geraldine Fielding a week ago had settled. But the team was still somewhat buoyed up by their success. He should be sharing those feelings with them, but the black mood that had settled since his disagreement with Loveday was still with him. He shouldn't have said those things. He'd handled it badly. He should have been more humble and talked of his concern for her safety out on the cliffs that day. Explained his anger was mainly with himself for not being there. Why hadn't he? He didn't know.

He'd driven up to Plymouth on Sunday. They weren't expecting him. Victoria's new partner was there. But Maddie and Jack had been excited to see

301

him and pleaded with him to join them for the Sunday Roast. But Victoria's eyes had said '*Don't you dare accept.*' So he hadn't. Arrangements were made for him to collect the children the following Friday night and bring them to Cornwall for the weekend. And this time he wouldn't be letting them down — no matter what. The feeling of lethargy had stayed with him on the drive back to Stithians after his fall out with Loveday that afternoon. Pictures of her kept flitting through his mind: her poor scratched face, the bruises. They made her look vulnerable. Wasn't it his job to protect the public? But then Loveday wasn't just another punter. But why did she have to be so headstrong?

Sam had never been inside the Truro Register Office. It was on the other side of town. He'd thought of walking, and then changed his mind. The air had a nip in it now, signs of the approaching Cornish winter.

'Sam!' Charlie interrupted his nervous pacing to rush forward, hand outstretched in greeting. 'Thank god you've come. I need some moral support here.'

Sam glanced over his shoulder into the room where the ceremony would take place. It was a sea of pinks and fuchsias, lemons and powder blues, interspersed with the more sombre colours of the male wedding guests.

'They're all Laura's friends,' he explained, flapping his hand towards the gathering. 'You see that little group down at the front?'

Sam strained his neck and nodded when he saw the half dozen people in the far away corner.

'That's all of my lot.'

Sam smiled and put a hand on Charlie's back. He could feel his friend trembling. 'Nerves are normal,' he assured with a pat. 'Just look at the bride you're getting.' He beamed across the foyer as Laura approached. She was wearing a fetching cream dress and matching jacket and carrying a neat bouquet of tiny pink roses and trailing gypsophilia.

'You look just wonderful,' he said, embracing her. 'You both do.'

'You'll be joining us at the reception?'

Charlie asked, his eyes pleading. 'It's at Trevarthian Manor.'

That hadn't been part of Sam's plan, but giving up an afternoon for his friend surely wasn't too much to ask. So he nodded. 'Of course I'm coming,' he said. 'Wouldn't miss it.'

'Great. We're just waiting for Laura's friend, then we can go in.' Charlie's hands were still visibly shaking.

'Here she is now,' Laura smiled as the newcomer approached. Sam spun round and found himself staring into Loveday's blue eyes.

She touched her still bruised cheek with an embarrassed smile. 'Not great for the wedding photos. I'll have to steer clear of the photographer.'

Sam was unprepared for the little flutter of pleasure that had started inside him. 'I didn't know you were coming . . . you . . . you didn't say.'

'Well, inspector,' she said, keeping her expression blank, 'Maybe you'll just have to accept that you don't know everything.'

Bride and groom exchanged uneasy glances. But Loveday had produced a little bunch of white heather. 'Special delivery from the Highlands,' she said. 'My mother sent it for luck.'

She handed the little posy to Laura, but not before extracting a sprig.

Turning to Sam, she tucked the prickly heather into the lapel of his jacket and gave it a little pat. 'Would have looked better on the tweed one,' she said, struggling to keep a straight face as his eyes narrowed in a look that said he hoped he wasn't misunderstanding the gesture.

But as they walked into the Marriage Room, Loveday hadn't missed Sam's smile. His day had suddenly improved.

THE END

We do hope that you have enjoyed reading this large print book.

Did you know that all of our titles are available for purchase?

We publish a wide range of high quality large print books including:
Romances, Mysteries, Classics
General Fiction
Non Fiction and Westerns

Special interest titles available in large print are:
The Little Oxford Dictionary
Music Book, Song Book
Hymn Book, Service Book

Also available from us courtesy of Oxford University Press:
Young Readers' Dictionary
(large print edition)
Young Readers' Thesaurus
(large print edition)

For further information or a free brochure, please contact us at:
Ulverscroft Large Print Books Ltd.,
The Green, Bradgate Road, Anstey,
Leicester, LE7 7FU, England.
Tel: (00 44) 0116 236 4325
Fax: (00 44) 0116 234 0205